W9-DES-297

Dixie Riggs

Also by Sarah Gilbert

HAIRDO

SARAH
GILBERT

A Time Warner Company

Jamie Raab, my friend, thank you.

Warner Books, Inc., 666 Fifth Avenue, New York, NY 10103
A Time Warner Company

Printed in the United States of America
First Printing: March 1991
10 9 8 7 6 5 4 3 2 1

Library of Congress Cataloging-in-Publication Data

Gilbert, Sarah.
Dixie Riggs / Sarah Gilbert.
p. cm.
ISBN 0-446-51527-2
I. Title.
PS3557.I34228.D5 1991
813'.54—dc20

90-50536
CIP

Book design by Giorgetta Bell McRee

With love for Momma who, thank goodness,
didn't raise me in any L-shaped rooms.

And with love for Kathy, Micah and Adam
and all those hot nights we spent together
in the Maple Street Maze without an air conditioner.

And for Sue, too.

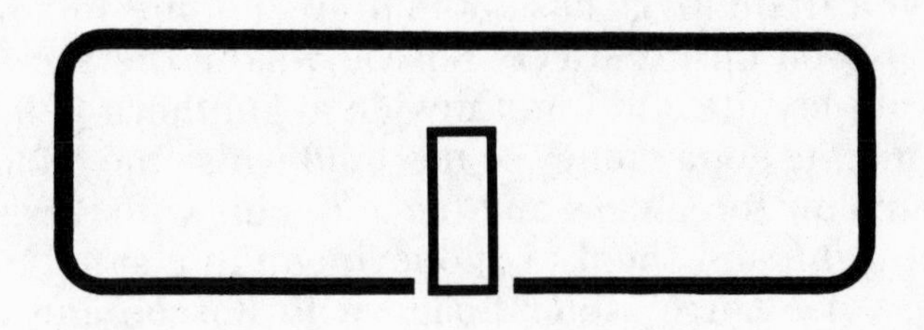

People always ask me the same question. They say, "Dixie Riggs, you are so good looking. Did you always want to be a model?" I always lie. I always tell them that I come from a long string of people in the beauty business. That my mother was a model and my father was an actor, and my aunts and uncles styled wigs for the town theater. But the truth of the matter is, none of that was true. I always just wanted to be married. But Buck Speed would not have me. So one day I walked out of his parents' house where I was living, in the center of the center of Myrtle Beach, South Carolina, and signed up for modeling school for two hundred dollars. But first let me back up all the way to the beginning and tell you about me and Buck.

Before and during Buck there were others. Like I had the biggest crush on this boy named Lance. He had long hair and a tattoo of the Tasmanian Devil on his arm which turned all kinds of neat colors when he got a tan. You wouldn't have liked him. Still, I did, so I asked around and found out that he had dropped out of high school. Can I pick them or what? We hung out together for a few weeks and two good suntans until I found out that he had been kicked out of his house at sixteen, married at seventeen, and was still married when we were swimming together down by the Pavilion. Can I pick a winner? Lance told me he was getting separated, but still. Even Dixie Riggs has got to draw the line somewhere.

So I moved on to Roscoe. Roscoe was in the service. He came into my life and I quit my job at Southern Bell where I was making good money so he could whisk me off to some California air force base and make me his wife. Yes, I married all right, and spent my honeymoon in a small room at the Casa del Zorro Motor Lodge with Roscoe and Private First Class somebody. While Roscoe and I consummated our marriage under the velveteen pictures of the cacti plants, Private First Class sat on the floor and watched TV with the lights out. After that, they left to go play pool. The next day I spent trying to find Roscoe, the next night I spent listening to the motel attendant getting stabbed, and the next day after that, while Roscoe was heading for AWOL, I was on an army transport bus, courtesy of the chaplain's office, heading as far away from San Diego as I could get—home to a Georgia annulment. I can really pick them, can't I?

So when Buck Speed came into my life, I was ready for a little serenity. Some peace and quiet was all I really needed. Buck was nothing but peace and quiet and dreams. He was going to be everything, build everything, meet everybody, be a star. He was going to grease his wheels on the bodybuilding circuit and become Mr. Universe, making his name a household word. When he got famous enough, he would go into acting. Then, when he was truly famous, he was going to be an evangelist. A televangelist, bringing the name of the Lord right into you as you sat on your own sofa. I was in on the early stages of this planning, keeping a schedule for him, making him stick to it, cooking for him, cleaning for him. It was my job. The only one he would let me have. But still, Buck Speed would not marry me. He said that he wanted to have the kind of place a woman would be happy living in. He said that a man painting cars was not the kind of man a woman needed to be marrying. He said a lot of things.

So I had this huge problem. Not just something you laugh at. Me and Buck were living at his momma and daddy's. Buck was sanding and painting cars and dreaming of whatever, and meanwhile I was sunning out by the pier, picking up all kinds of boys even though I wanted nothing to do with any of them. It's just that I can never tell a boy no. At first it was all right. I could just go on off with my bottle of Captain Jack Hawaiian Suntan Oil, slather it on and bronze away in my bikini, having myself a good old time. I'd come home a little late with the excuse that I'd fallen asleep in the sun, or that I'd run into Sparkle, my best friend. I'd put on an apron and help Buck's momma with the cooking and everything went as pretty as you please. Buck was happy, his momma was happy, his daddy was watching TV so I guess he was happy. And my female hormones had been temporarily soothed, so I was temporarily happy too. But then the boys started phoning over to Buck's looking for me and it didn't take a genius to see that it was time for me to make a move.

So here's the deal: I'm sitting on the sofa with Buck's daddy, after a particularly uncomfortable dinner where I had managed to pretend that two possible disastrous phone calls from boys were really calls from my best friend Sparkle. I'd smile at Buck and his daddy and momma and say into the phone to one boy, "Oh hey, Sparkle. Listen here now, there's no way I can go out tonight. You understand what I'm saying here. I can't go anywhere." The words would come out all strangled. Meanwhile the Speeds would be eating in silence, as always, shaking their heads at Sparkle again. And then another call would come in and I'd jump to answer it and it would be another boy and I'd say, "Sparkle, listen here, hon. You just got to quit calling me. I'm trying to eat, and no, I cannot go out." It was a mess.

Anyway, there I am on the sofa after dinner with Daddy Speed, as he's called, sitting on the edge of my seat to answer the phone in case it rings again, and I see this advertisement come on TV for modeling classes at Renee's World of Fashion Modeling. Well you can only imagine that right there and right then my interest, on a scale of 1 to 10, was registering a red hot 10! So I mailed off for the form.

A few days later the information comes in the morning mail. I see the answer to all my problems. It comes to me like Bingo! I can fill up all this free time I have with six weeks of modeling school, thereby thinning out the interest these boys have in me. At the same time I can become a famous fashion model with no need for Buck Speed whatsoever. And won't he be begging me to marry him then, and I will just say a big "Sorrrrrry!"

I like this. I like this new way of thinking.

What I don't like is that the only class available is a six o'clock night basic. I can tell immediately that I don't want to be in this class. I want to be in the one with the professional girls because I know I am good looking enough. I know Myrtle Beach hasn't seen the likes of me since Vanna White, who is my idea of a good looking woman, hit the big time. I know that all it will take will be the right pair of eyes to discover me and I will be on my way. But it is Renee Dupree who is offering this class, and since Renee Dupree is the first person to have discovered Vanna White, there is no question that I will take the only class she has to offer.

So I jumped on into my Dodge Charger, the old yellow one that Buck has been promising to paint metallic blue all summer long, and went on down to the Scissor Wizard Beauty Shop to grab Sparkle, who, on a good day, really is my best friend. She was in the back giving her momma, Trina Starling, the owner of the shop, a manicure, saying, "You'll never in a million years believe what Dixie told me the other day. Said she was going to be a model. A *famous* model. Well, ha ha. If Dixie Riggs can pass a modeling course, I'm short and fat."

Her momma cracked up laughing.

It beat all. There I was twenty-two years old on a motorcycle heading for forty, living with my boyfriend's parents, with them and me wondering if Buck and me were ever going to be married, and it wasn't the fact that Sparkle, who by the way is skinny, skinny and five eleven in her stocking feet, said I couldn't pass the course. It was just the way she said it. It was the same way she was always talking about Buck and what a no-good fool he was, that made me turn right back around out that front door and spend the rest of the day charging up a whole new modeling wardrobe at

Newberry's Department Store with Buck's momma's credit card. It didn't even occur to me until after I'd bought everything I'd wanted that I'd never be able to pay her back. I mean, I'd saved up *some* money from my job at Southern Bell but not *that* much. Maybe sixty or seventy dollars for gas and Tampax and such. Of course I could've tried returning the items, but by then I was so in love with every little thing that there was just no turning back. That's what I meant when I said I had this huge problem.

2

By the next day I had forgiven Sparkle for her mean and nasty ways. I hate her and I love her and that is just the kind of relationship we have. What I had done was to spend the morning laying out in the sun in my new orange Day-Glo rubber French-cut bathing suit with the wide frontal zipper, flirting with these two really good looking lifeguards, and I was ready to be friends again. So I dropped back into the Scissor Wizard and there was Sparkle, styling her snooty mother's hair.

And I said, "Sparkle, we've got to talk."

And she said, "You bet we do. Listen here girl, you think you could do me a favor and take some pictures of me?"

And I said, "Sure. Why?"

And she said, "Well, there's this guy, you see, and he's in the air force and Dix, he's really cute."

This is exactly what Sparkle is like when she is not busy bad-mouthing me. She is always talking about men. She has dated almost every man in town. Probably her longest record for being with any man is six weeks. She says that as soon as they get comfortable enough to leave their socks on the floor, she hits the road. She says there is nothing worse than a bore, and that there is no bore worse than Buck, who she says is a bore's bore. Sparkle cannot stand Buck.

He in turn says that Sparkle is an ungodly woman and a sleaze and that if I have to hang around her, he'd rather not know about it. This is partly because it is true, partly because I've used her so many times as my alibi. Anyway, it doesn't take a genius to see that these two won't ever make "The Dating Game."

Sparkle went on to tell me that this guy had not called her for days. "Dixie," she said, "he won't call me until I get him the pictures."

"What kind of pictures are we talking about, hon?" I asked, suspicious. She was still working with her mother's hair, trying to make it stand tall with the miracle of hairspray.

Her momma sighed impatiently at me and said, "I swear, Dixie, get with it. Naked pictures, of course."

And I went, "Naked pictures?"

And Sparkle said, "Momma says they'll make him mad with desire. It was her idea."

Sparkle's momma, Trina, just patted her hand for her to go on fixing her hair. So being the good friend that I am, I said, "Hon, I don't think you need to be going out with a creep like that."

"Oh Dixie," she said. She rolled her eyes at me and handed her momma a blue plastic hand mirror. Her mother picked at the top of her hair to make it stand up more like a rock star's and Sparkle said, "Sometimes I'd swear that you had no savvy about you. Don't you ever just feel like cutting loose and posing in something sexy for Buck for a change?"

It was the very last thing I felt like. If Buck thought I was even *feeling* that way he'd drag me, a raised Methodist, down to the Ocean Highway Baptist Church and make me get down on my knees and get saved three times. Once Buck and me were watching this funny movie. There was this scene in it where this couple is making love. The man puts a pillow under the woman's behind. Well I started laughing because it was a comedy and all, but Buck, he was furious at me. He turned that TV right off and lectured me, then interrogated me. Boy did he ever interrogate me, all night long and into the dawn about who I'd done that with before and when and where and didn't I know it was a sin? Now I can barely watch the old reruns of "The Love Boat" without him hovering over me waiting to get mad.

I guess Trina knew what I was thinking about because she said, "Ha! Buck Speed? Posing sexy for Buck Speed? You've got to be kidding Sparkle. He's too much of a drip."

Sparkle laughed and said, "Tell me about it. I must've lost my head there for a minute."

And so choosing to ignore them, I said, "Sparkle, you want to start modeling school with me?"

And she said, "No, Dixie, no I really don't think so."

And then I said, "Why?"

And then she said, "What could they teach me that I don't already know?"

"How about everything, you conceited little bitch," is what I felt like saying, but instead I just said, "Oh come on, Sparkle. Give it a shot. It'll be fun."

And so she said, "Okay Dixie, sure. But on one condition."

And I said, "What's that girl?"

And she said, "Are you going to take those naked shots of me, or what?"

Right off the bat, I know one person who would not be caught dead posing in the nude. Her name is Paulette. I do not like to talk about her. I cannot stand her and I cannot stand that name. I have never met her, but I see her every day of my life. Her picture hangs above Buck's bed. She has sleek brown hair and one laughing brown eye that knows something. Her other eye is hidden beneath a red hat that is cocked to the side. Her lips are red, too, but not as red as the anger that consumes me every time I see her. I want to take her by the shoulders and shake her down hard and say, "You are not as good looking as you think you are you little slut," but instead I just let this madness fester inside me.

And I say, "Buck, it feels really weird us making love with her watching over our heads like that."

And he breathes in sharply and says through his clenched teeth, "Dixie," like he has done a hundred times before. We have this conversation a lot.

And I say, "But Buck, you could always take it down, you know."

And then he starts clipping his words short and says, "It's just a picture, Dix."

And I say, "Yeah, but it's a picture of *her*."

Then he goes on to explain in a very exasperated manner

that it is an art shot, a professional picture out of her modeling portfolio, and he just likes it is all and is that such a crime? And since he loves me, not her, and since she doesn't even live in the same town anymore, it really shouldn't matter. But I know for a fact that even though she doesn't live here, she flies in whenever she wants to because she is, after all, a Pan American flight attendant, something I myself would kill to be.

I go to bed at night thinking of her strolling up and down the aisle of a 747 offering every man she meets scotch and peanuts. She's got on a cute little Pan Am uniform, but she still has that red hat cocked over her eye, and she's still smiling. I am convinced that Buck has the exact same vision before he goes to sleep, so I toss it and turn it around in my brain while I toss and turn in my bed until I am ragged.

My only consolation is that she wanted to be a model but ended up being a stewardess. This is one very good reason why it is so important for me to go on to modeling school. The only possible way to conquer this obsession with Paulette is for me to become the famous model she failed to be. Then and only then will I be able to shake her up like she has shaken me.

Finally, to get to sleep, I envision myself on that plane with her coming up the aisle pushing her shining silver cart, stopping dead in her tracks and saying, "Oh my God, it's Dixie Riggs! The Revlon cover girl!" She has her hand over her mouth in awe. Sometimes Buck is with me and she spots the large diamond on my wedding finger. Meanwhile, he doesn't even notice her. And sometimes, on a good night when I'm real, real strong, I'm sitting next to a movie producer who is dangling a Cartier pearl necklace from his hand for me to wear. But I just ignore him and smile sweetly at her and feel sorry for her because I notice her ankles are all big and swollen from all those nights of walking up and down and up and down the plane's aisle.

I cross my own skinny ankles under the covers and then, and only then, am I finally able to fall asleep.

Momma Speed is the only woman I know who still wears baloney curls. You know, the kind where clumps of hair are teased up, then rolled around your finger? You clip them right on the base of the roller, stacking one on top of the other. Then, when you take them down they come falling down like a waterfall—a cascade of Shirley Temple curls. I'd been trying to break her out of that 'do for months, but she said Mr. Speed didn't want any big changes.

That would describe Mr. Speed in a nutshell. It's hard to imagine that Buck came from that man. Where Buck's such a dreamer, Mr. Speed is all business. He thinks Buck is a mess. Here's an example of Mr. Speed. One time I had a little cookout in their backyard for Sparkle and Trina and they brought a cousin along. Well I know for a fact that Mr. Speed hasn't stopped looking at girls. He has stacks and stacks of girlie magazines in his garage.

Anyway, I saw him giving Sparkle's cousin the once-over more than once. He had the funniest look on his face. He also had a pair of pliers in his hand. Mr. Speed always has some kind of garden tool or something in his hand. So there he was, squeezing those pliers, and Sparkle walked by. He touched her arm with the tip of his pliers and said, "She's the tallest woman I've ever seen," talking about Sparkle's cousin, of course.

And Sparkle said to him, because she just couldn't help herself, she said, "She's had the sex change. She comes to my house now and pees all over the toilet. She used to be called Lester but now we just call her Leslie."

Sparkle told me later that he squeezed those pliers as tight as his teeth were clenched and said, "Me and her would've had a fight if I'd have woken up to her that next morning and found out she used to be Lester."

Needless to say, there never really was any such a thing as a Lester, because Leslie's been a girl ever since she and Sparkle were little girls sharing Barbie dolls. And Sparkle, being the kind of girl she is, never did clear this matter up with Mr. Speed, who still walks around talking about "that *thang*" walking around in "*his* house," and there has not been a backyard barbecue since at the Speeds'.

It's weird when you think about it. About me living with Buck and his momma and daddy. They had their room and I shared with Buck. He had a room right off the kitchen with no door, just a curtain. The first time I saw that, I didn't feel too good. But you get to where you get used to things.

When I first met Buck it was on that transport bus coming out of my marriage. He was coming home from a discharge and happy to be coming home. Anyway, I'd say we were in love before we pulled into the terminal. Boy, was he ever a passionate one then. It was like "Dixie, I want you to marry me, I want you to be my wife, but I don't want you to work because whoever heard of a televangelist's wife working as an operator?" So within the week I had packed up from Cordele, Georgia, where my family was, and moved to Myrtle Beach, S.C., where I have been living with him ever since.

Buck's momma was the first to greet me at that front door on that first day. She wore about thirty pink sponge curlers in her hair. Mr. Speed was standing not ten feet behind her, with a skinny little necktie bulging his neck. He was tuning his guitar. Their faces were just shining. Momma Speed got behind her Hammond organ and Buck's daddy started picking out a song that he had written special just for me. I don't have to tell you that it worked like magic. I knew right then that Buck's family was the one for me.

Anyway, all this is background on what my home life was like. I say "was" because the music stopped just as soon as the realization came over Momma and Daddy Speed that Buck wasn't going to marry me. Dinners started getting a little quieter. Momma Speed stopped taking me to meet all the cousins. Mr. Speed didn't pick on me like he used to. I moved out of Buck's room into the sewing room. It didn't have a picture of Paulette. It had a door. Buck had started saying that it wasn't right for a televangelist to be sharing his bed with a woman who wasn't even his wife yet.

I'd say, "But Buck, we could always get married, you know," because getting married was all I ever wanted in the whole wide world.

And he'd say, "Yes, but first I've got to build us a house. We can't be married and living with my momma at the same time."

And I'd say, "But Buck, you haven't even finished putting in the door to your room. What makes you think you are going to build us a house?"

And he'd say, "That's different. How can I spend money on our house if I have to use it to fix up Momma's?"

He had a point there. But that point kept getting smaller and smaller until I could plainly see that there was no house in the future for me and Buck. That's when the boys began to sense my need for attention and started gathering around me at the beach.

I'm only human. When Buck's best friend Donnie Sessions came around with that cute little cleft in his chin, and Buck was too busy sanding a 1958 pickup truck to be painted candy apple red, I went out on a motorcycle ride with Donnie. Unfortunately, that ride lasted through the weekend.

Believe you me, that was one tough entrance to make into Buck's house the day I did come back.

Momma Speed sat me down and fixed me lunch like she always did. She didn't say a word or act any more mopey than she already had been acting ever since our wedding plans had taken a 180-degree turn for the worst. Buck's daddy came in from out of the garage carrying a pair of wire cutters and a piece of rubber-coated wire. While I ate, he stripped the rubber off the wire, then he cut it into three lengths. Then to clinch it, Buck came in and said, "Well, hey stranger," not at all mad.

It was spooky. It has been that way now for nearly three weeks and still nobody has said a word about that missing weekend to me. I guess that was my deciding factor in needing to move out and get me my own place. But how I was going to do it was going to be another thing. I hadn't worked since I was a Southern Bell operator and Buck had promised me his never-ending support and love on that Trailways bus. And even though he really didn't support me, his momma and daddy did. Because of them I was eating good food, sleeping on clean sheets, and once in a while I even got to go to a movie. But sometimes a woman's just got to have enough strength and power to leave a man if she's not getting the kind of attention she needs, or the clothes she needs. Which brings me back to my problem of money. Pretty soon even my gas money would go. It had already dwindled down to a lousy fifty dollars! And Lord, when that bill came from the department store stating that I owed the limit on Buck's momma's credit card, well, I couldn't even think about that. Not to mention that on top of that, I owed Buck's momma rent, a little thing that Buck just happened to have mentioned to me one night after I happened to have mentioned our postponed wedding plans just one more time.

So when Renee Dupree's school of modeling asked me if I had the two hundred dollars for the registration fee, it was one of the faster lies I jumped on. I was not about to lose my one-way ticket out of this nonmarriage. I was not about to lose a career. I said, "Of course I have two hundred dollars."

It's just like Sparkle always says, "Dixie Riggs, I may be a slut, but I don't believe you have even a nodding acquaintance with the truth."

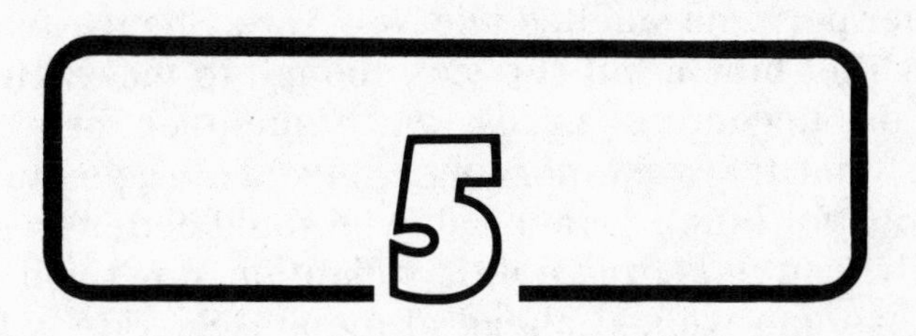

If men only knew how little it took to make women happy they would die. This was the case with Buck Speed and me. If Buck had just said, "Dixie, girl, I love you so much and if you'll just stay home and sweep my floors for the rest of your natural born life, I will marry you," I would have said yes in a heartbeat. But Buck hadn't said a thing.

So six o'clock sharp found me and Sparkle passing the old Pavilion and then the new Pavilion, not taking a right off the Ocean Boulevard to get off at the beach as we usually did—to flirt with all the good looking boys there—but taking a left down a small dirt road that led to Renee Dupree's World of Fashion Modeling. It was nestled in between two dead live oaks outside a house called "Pellican's Perch" and a house called "Dun Cum Home" with no dead live oaks but two palmetto trees. It was as pink as a house could be. It looked like Pepto Bismol to Sparkle. It looked like heaven to me.

Up on the roof was a sign turning around and around at a slant, blinking MODEL MODEL MODEL over and over again in bright blue neon. I knew the minute I saw it I was going to be famous.

We knocked and then rang and then pounded on the door, and finally a tall overdressed woman let us in. She had all the right modeling moves, all the right modeling clothes, even her perfume smelled like New York. She wasn't Renee, I knew that much, but she was enough to make me forget about my upcoming success and remember instead Buck saying to me that very morning as I fixed me a peanut butter sandwich for lunch, "Honey, maybe you'd better go slow on the jelly. You're getting a little weight on, don't you think?"

The woman walked ahead of me and Sparkle, who ourselves were dressed to the bones, leading us to a room where seven other girls, all equally nervous, were smiling at one another, sitting on a long T-shaped runway. She pointed her dagger-red fingernails at a spot on the very end of the runway and said, "Sit there." Then she turned around and floated out the door.

The girl sitting next to me wasn't used to wearing dresses. It was in the crossing and recrossing of her legs, the way she hugged her knees as she did so. Sparkle eyed her and said real loud, because Sparkle is like this, "God, I wouldn't be caught dead wearing polyester."

And I said, "Shut up, Sparkle."

And she said, "How do you like my outfit?"

And I said, "I don't."

And she said, "That's just because you're jealous."

But I wasn't, really. Sparkle dresses like a drag queen. She always wears these flowery, flowing dresses that look like they belong in a Kotex commercial, on a girl much smaller than herself. I, on the other hand, was getting my confidence back. I knew I looked good, wearing my sequined tube top with a black leather skirt and an imitation rabbit fur coat. I don't believe in wearing real furs. I also had on high heels, but not too high. I didn't want to look like a hooker. One thing about me, I know how to take things as far as they can go before they shouldn't go any further. I'm good like that. So there we all were, sizing each other up, knowing that there wasn't a chance in hell that this girl would make it or that girl would, unless of course this one could just lose those hips, or that one could get thicker hair or a thinner face, and then maybe, just maybe, they might have a chance but thank God they didn't, when suddenly I got my first sight of Renee

Dupree. You didn't just see Renee, you feasted your eyes on her as she glided into the room on some invisible wheels. She checked her watch, said, "Oh, phooey on myself, late again," laughed, put a finger to her cheek and surveyed her new girls.

And that's when she started in with the no, huh-uh, no, not that! "No, little darling," she'd say. "No, that won't do." She was much different than I had pictured her. I thought for sure she would have frizzy red hair and an attitude about her, like her picture in the brochure. Instead she had soft blond hair with an old-fashioned pageboy flip and a way about her. There was just something about her that let you know that she knew everything, that she knew fame.

She went straight up to Sparkle, lifting the sleeve of her dress. As it flowed back down she said, "Honey, this is something you'd wear to an aunt's second wedding. Next time you come in here, you're going to be dressed like someone on the cover of *Mademoiselle* magazine."

Everyone laughed real nervous and then she said, "No, and you there, you with that fur on. Think seasonal, hon. Seasonal. What may be in style in the winter does not necessarily hold true for the spring."

It didn't take a genius to see that she was talking about me. Even if Sparkle hadn't nudged me, I was the only one she could have been talking about. I knew Miss Dupree was right about my fake fur, but it had been on sale during my little Newberry's Department Store spree and it was a cool night anyway. But we learned about that too.

"Little darlings, let me tell you the first thing about dressing. Even if it is snowing, when that calender turns over to spring, you best remember to jump into your cottons or you might as well just keep your daytime job. Modeling is a business just like any other business. And just like any other business, sometimes you have to do things you don't want to."

She told us to call her Renee. Then she went up to every girl, one at a time, and said no to everything everyone had on, and as quick as she did this, she said, "Okay. The first thing I'm going to teach my little Renettes is how to sit. There are three ways, and three ways only. From now on, whoever does not sit this way in class will get points taken off. It is very, very important to have as many points as you can, so we can hire you for the agency when you graduate."

Looking back on it now, I must say that those next hours were the most excruciating hours I had ever spent sitting in my entire life. We could either cross our legs at the ankle, or cross our calf above our knee just so long as we didn't rest it there pushing the flesh in an unattractive way, or, lastly, we could keep both legs together, side by side, either to the right or the left of us, making sure to keep our feet on tippytoes. I went for that. Sparkle, on the other hand, kept pressing her calf against her knee and getting in trouble for it.

"Young lady!" Renee would say, clapping her hands up in the air in Sparkle's direction, and that's all she would say.

It was like everything I had ever heard basic training in the army was like. But I loved every minute of it. We all did. We were on our way to becoming models. When it became too painful to sit with my back so straight, I'd look at the posters on the walls of all the models who had made it before me and think to myself, "They are much, much prettier than that stupid Paulette. And just think, in seven or eight weeks I'll probably be running up Park Avenue with them, doing a gig for *Glamour* magazine or *Vogue*, and then won't Buck Speed ever be crying in his soup. I bet he'll take her picture down then."

Then I had a little scare. Renee said, "For any of you who are over nineteen, we'll be teaching you how to wear makeup for everyday use. For those of you who are younger, I'll teach you how to do it the model way."

As soon as she said it, the woman who had led us in was back in with us, standing over us, studying us.

And Renee said, "Little Renettes, this is Casey. She's my assistant. Casey is five ten and wears a perfect size eight. Casey, weed them out."

I did not want to be weeded out, but Casey was looking hard at my twenty-two-year-old face, saying, "Is there anyone here who is older than nineteen?"

Sparkle pressed against me hard and I pressed back. The girl next to us was pushing an easy thirty, but she was keeping her hand down too.

"Dixie," whispered Sparkle, flipping her blond hair off her shoulders, "what are we going to do?"

I pulled my long coal black hair in front to frame my face and whispered back, "Shut up, Sparkle."

Casey pointed at us. "Young ladies?"

And I said, "I'm nineteen."

Sparkle, who was always a dead giveaway in a lie, said, "Me, too."

And the girl next to me said, "Me, too," in a small, thin voice.

Casey went from staring us down long and hard to completely destroying this other girl by saying, "More like twenty-seven. If that. Darling, they wouldn't even think about taking you in New York." She turned to Renee and said, "Day makeup."

Renee checked her list.

Then Casey looked back at me and Sparkle one more time before she went on to the next girl and grilled her. By the time we had all filed into the makeup room, four of the girls had been checked as day makeup and you could tell they felt bad. I felt bad for them.

"In front of you," said Renee, "you will all find sponges and makeup. I want you to try the foundations on your wrist and the one that most suits your coloring, that's what I want you to put on your face. Use upward strokes, girls, upward strokes. Casey will be back in to help you directly. In the meantime, Casey, can I talk to you a moment, puh-lease."

"Puh-lease" sounded like trouble to me. They left the room and, as we worked, we could hear them whispering in the next room. There are whispers and there are whispers. And these, I was sure, were trouble whispers. I was sweating out them being whispers about me and how I should be day makeup, too, and why hadn't Casey picked up on this. So I packed on the concealer. And I packed me on some more. And then Casey came in looking the same as when she'd gone out, unaffected, and told me to take some off. Then she went up to each girl and told them all kinds of neat beauty hints, such as a little dab of Vaseline on your teeth makes your smile shine brighter. And if you don't have any eyebrows to speak of, brush them with brown mascara. And if you put on creme blush before powder blush, it will blend in better. Stuff like that.

At least a half hour passed before Renee finally came back. My face felt like wet cardboard, dried. My eyes, with four coats of mascara on them, felt like I had Christmas trees for eyelashes. Sparkle really looked like a drag queen now. She had chosen a heavy peach foundation and she looked sick and orange. Most of the other girls looked like they had been scared or, worse, sold to a circus. But we felt beautiful. And Renee made us believe we were. "Oh my little Renettes, you all are gorgeous! And you know, most girls have to stay on with us through advanced and professional classes, but something tells me we have one or two stars in here already, who will be signing up with Eileen Ford before the six weeks are up. Oh," she said, clasping her hands together, "this is going to be a model class. A model class."

And I swear, I think she even started to cry.

When we walked out of there, we were all carrying over sixty-five dollars' worth of new World of Modeling Cosmetics, because Renee had said, "If you want to be a model, you must first use what the models use. This, my little sugars, is the only makeup they use in New York City."

It's funny when you think about it. What a woman will do, I mean. For instance, one minute I was leaving modeling school with Renee reminding me I owed two hundred dollars for classes plus the makeup I'd just put on credit, and the next minute I was behind a camera taking pictures of Sparkle pushing her breasts up at me. She kept saying, "Oooh, do you like it? Do you like it?" I guess she meant it for this mystery boyfriend of hers, but it was too weird for me, so I said, "Sparkle, you're going to have to be quiet if you want me to do this."

But she was already too far gone, sprawling her naked body through the eye of the camera into her air force boy's heart, with me acting like I'm just taking pictures of trees or something. But here's the really strange thing, the really Sparkle-type thing: we were doing it in her momma's boyfriend's apartment.

Now don't get me wrong, neither her mother or the boyfriend were anywhere in sight. I hadn't even met this guy, did not even know his name. But I could tell you an awful lot about him just by the way he decorated his apartment. There was grass wallpaper on every wall, just like they have in the dentist office. All his furniture matched perfectly and was perfectly ugly. Everything was tan Naugahyde—the color of the crayon you'd never take out of the box when you were a kid—flesh colored. And of course, everything L-shaped into everything else. The couch L-shaped into a love seat which L-shaped into the kitchen, which had an island that L-shaped into the direction of the hall, which L-shaped right on into the bathroom, then the bedroom where Sparkle and I were. Now me, I've always thought this kind of setup was all wrong. You walk into a place like this and it's as if there's some kind of set pattern you've got to follow. Such as: You walk in. You turn on the TV. You go to the kitchen. You fix yourself a little dinner. You eat it. Then you go into the bathroom and brush your teeth, then go to sleep. Then, you wake up, shave, go back to work, and before you know it, you're back home again doing the same old L-shaped cycle.

Well, when Sparkle told me Trina's beau was in insurance, I was not a bit surprised. Neither was I when I saw that the bed Sparkle was sprawled across had black satin sheets on it, flat and fitted. It is just like an L-shaped man to own a seedy looking bedroom like that. Naked pictures would be no strangers to this man's room.

I said, "Grab that pillow, Sparkle, honey." It was a black satin heart-shaped pillow. "And cover up your noonie. We want to leave something to the imagination. That's good."

I was beginning to get worried. Not only was I taking pictures of her, I was directing her too. And I was enjoying myself. "Sparkle," I'd say, "now move your left leg a little to the right and, yes, that's it, and bring your right foot up to meet the other thigh. No, right foot hon, good."

We took twenty-four shots of Sparkle sliding on the bed, pushing her breasts up and out at the camera, her lips smooched into the perfect pout. She had what every great porn star has, whatever that is. She was a pro at crawling around on her knees. Suddenly I got this great idea. It was something I had always wanted to do, something I had read about in one of Buck's daddy's girlie magazines where they swear that they do not airbrush the model. Instead, they contour her cleavage with a dark blusher to make it look deeper.

Using some of the World of Modeling makeup we had just

purchased from Renee, I did this to Sparkle. Then I brushed the entire breast with World of Modeling pearly white eye shadow. This was to make them look big and voluptuous. But the other part I made Sparkle do herself. “Sparkle,” I said, “you are going to have to take one of these lipsticks and circle each nipple. Which color you want?”

“The pink one.”

“Pink is for the prom. Let’s try this red instead.”

There are two kinds of people in this world. Ones that can draw a perfect circle and then there’s ones that can’t. Sparkle, as it turned out, couldn’t. So I ended up having to do that, too, which in itself is very strange. Especially doing it to a girl I’d known for less than a year. Especially doing it to a girl I’d met trying to pick up the same lifeguard I was. I don’t know. It was strange.

After Sparkle’s makeover, as we called it, I ran her a bubble bath. She stuck her foot in and then right back out and said, “Ohhh Dixie, it’s freezing!”

“I know.”

“What do you mean, you know? I’m not about to get in there.”

“Sparkle. Come on. It has to be cold to, well, you know.”

“No. I’m not getting back in there like that. We’ll have to warm it up first.” She turned the hot water on full blast and I reached over and turned it right back off.

I was exasperated with her. “Sparkle,” I yelled. “It makes your nipples hard. Get it?”

She said, “I don’t care what it does, it’s pure double-T freezing in there.”

“Remember Roy?” Roy, I had found out, was the air force man’s name.

She said, “Oh glory, all right. This is for you, Roy, baby,” and got in very slowly, slowly going *ooooooo* the whole way in.

We only took twelve shots of her like that. Then it got too cold so we took our little act into the living room. I bent over the camera, away from the light, and reloaded it while Sparkle pulled something out from under the sofa.

“Don’t look, Dixie. This is going to crack you up.”

"Okay."

And she began laughing. Sparkle has the great laugh of all time. Every time she laughs I have to laugh too, just hearing her. So she's laughing and making all of this noise and I just can't stand it any longer so I turn around. There on the rug wiggled something like fifteen or twenty dicks. Well, vibrators shaped like somebody out there in vibrator land thinks dicks ought to be shaped. There were short fat red ones, spiked and curved ones, long long oh so long black ones; there were ones with faces on them; and there was even one with two heads, all surrounded by dozens of pieces of exotic lingerie. And Sparkle had turned them all onto high speed. They were heading towards me like snakes slithering across the rug. I screamed, "Oh gross, they're ugly. Get them away!"

Sparkle was laughing. And then she began picking them up and talking with them like they were puppets.

I won't go all into what she had them saying. It isn't important. But the bottom line is, they were telling her which little outfits to wear.

"Where did you get all this stuff?" I asked, amazed.

She said, "Me? They're Momma's. She sells them." She held up the vibrator with the face on it and said, in her best vibrator voice, "Sparkle, I think you should try on the black thing with the matching gloves."

She grabbed the curved one. "No, no," she said in the high, curvy voice of a vibrator, "it has to be the leopard panties, or nothing at all."

"I already have on nothing at all," she said back to it.

I was cracking up, taking pictures of her whole routine. Then she turned and jiggled the biggest vibrator of all at me, the long dark one, and said, "What do you say, Dixie? What's it going to be for you? A pair of these maybe?" She put the pair of leopard panties on her head like a hat.

I could barely move. I was laughing so hard. "There is no *way*, Sparkle!"

But she was right. One thing about Sparkle, she knows me better than I know myself. See, don't for one teeninsy little second let any woman on this planet earth tell you she isn't interested in wearing this kind of stuff or at least interested in trying it on. I'm just the type that would try to tell you that too. But even me, Dixie Riggs, couldn't wait to see what I'd look like in the mirror wearing that cute little red garter belt with the matching push-up bra.

"Whoa, Dixie, you look great!" Sparkle had put down the vibrator for the camera.

"No, Sparkle, don't do that," I said, laughing nervously.

"Come on girl. Let's get you up on that bed. That red stuff will look great against the black sheets. Here, put these on first." She threw a pair of satin red elbow-length fingerless gloves at me. They had a lace inseam.

I said, "Oh all right, but just for one shot. And keep those yukky things away from me," pointing to the vibrators. "Cover them up with a towel or something."

Now let me tell you, there are just some things I can't account for and one of those is why I do what I do sometimes. Like in a million years I wouldn't be able to explain to you why I walked back into that bedroom and started posing on that bed for my best friend Sparkle. I can only account for the time I spent. The first ten minutes I wore the red thing. Then I switched to the black thing. Then some pink hose and a pair of pasties with gold tassels, which wouldn't stay on because Sparkle had touched the gluey stuff and she was still a little wet from her bath. Then it was a black leather skirt that covered only half of my behind and a fringed cowboy jacket without the jacket, just the fringes dangling off my nipples. It was ridiculous. I felt ridiculous. And glory knows Sparkle was ridiculous standing there in her edible see-through panties and a cupless bra as she took picture after picture.

Holding my tassels out, laughing, I said, "This is the most insane-looking thing."

Sparkle said, "I know. But men love that kind of crap. Swang your thang, baby," she joked. "Come on, swang it." She started humming the striptease song, "Da dum dum, da dum dum, da dum dum, da da da da dum, da da da DUM, DUM," and there I was, swinging my thing to beat the band.

"Hold it. I've got a great idea," she said. "Come here."

I jumped off the bed and went over to where she was at and she flipped my head down, fluffed my hair out and said, "Okay Dixie, when I say so, I want you to flip your head back up with your lips in a full baby's pout, and say to me, 'Baby, you've just got to want some of this.' "

"I can't say that!" I shrieked, flipping my hair back.

"Keep going," she said, snapping away. "You look great, Dixie. Great."

"Sparkle *please*," I pleaded. I picked up the nearest thing, a strange looking kind of see-through girdle, to hide behind it, but when it hit my face I had to ask, "What is this?" I held it out and examined the label. It took a minute for it to sink in. "Oh my God! It's a pad-a-butt. Sparkle, it's a pad-a-butt. I got to try this on." I got back on the bed and squeezed into it. Then I really got silly. I ran to the living room and bounced on the sofa. "Sparkle look, it bounces!"

Sparkle just kept coming at me with the camera.

Pretty soon we were trading off, trading outfits, me in her leopard skins and her in my padded girdle, taking pictures of each other. I have never, even to this day, laughed so hard in my entire life. Sparkle was just so funny, especially when she put on a see-through apron and stood in front of the stove holding a pot, saying, "Hi, big boys. I'm Miss November. I like ponies, sports cars, men who don't curse, and I love to cook this way any chance I get. Yes, just say the words 'Campbell's soup' and you've got me for the rest of the night." She clanged the pot with a serving spoon and said, "Hey Dixie, I've got an idea. Let's get a picture of us together."

She grabbed the camera and set it up on the kitchen table facing the L-shaped sandwich bar and then she jumped up onto my naked lap. We were shrieking, waiting for the flash.

That's when we heard the front door. It was the old tried-and-true key-in-the-lock sound and it sent me knocking Sparkle off, hightailing it for the bedroom. Sparkle stayed frozen right where she was, on the floor looking horrified. I just about made it without being seen, but nobody is that lucky. The first thing I noticed about him was that he had the thinnest mustache I'd ever seen on a man. Why he had even bothered to wear one was beyond me. Well, it's just like me to get caught naked in some strange man's apartment thinking about his mustache. What I should have been thinking about was how my clothes were still in the living room and I had nothing else to put on but something of the boyfriend's or else another one of Trina's porno outfits. This is the kind of situation that only Dixie Riggs would find herself in. Other more normal women would be at home having dinner cooking on the stove for their husbands. But as you know, Buck Speed would not marry me, so here I was.

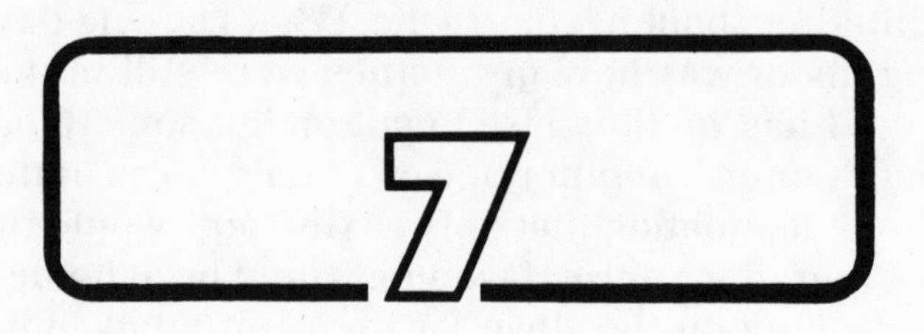

The whole thing got me all hot and bothered, having to sneak out of there like that with Sparkle and Trina's boyfriend having a little talk on his L-shaped sofa. I'd managed to get my clothes on and get out of there without being too obvious, but I'd put them on so fast, I'd forgotten to remove the last sexy outfit. It was the slinky leopard skin panties and nippleless bra. Like I said, I was really hot and bothered, so I pulled up to a Wing's Swim Wear "Nothing-over-a-Dollar" Store, and picked up the pay phone. Then I did what any red-blooded American woman would do at a time like that. I called Donnie Sessions.

There's no way to get to Donnie's except by going past the old Pavilion. Usually the night lights of the Ferris wheel and the roller coaster remind me of first week. Me and my girlfriends would drive the six hours over from Georgia. Myrtle Beach was the big place to be. We'd pick up boys and get in trouble. But for some reason, with the red and green and blue neon lights flashing at me, this night reminded me of something else, something I'd suspected all my life. That Myrtle Beach wasn't so big after all. That I was too good for a small town like this. And too good for a small town boy like Buck.

I rolled down my window and let the smell of cotton candy blow through my hair, and let the carnival music mix with the music on the car radio. Everything sounded confused, like the mixed-up stuff that was going around and around in my head like the Octopus Ride. I tried to tune it out, to think of something funny. So I thought about Donnie again. And like the snap of a finger I was back to my old happy self. So happy, in fact, that if somebody had come up to me in a cartoon strip and said in one frame, "Are you happy now, Dixie Riggs? You look mighty happy to me," I'd have been in the next frame with a balloon coming out of my mouth with the word "YES" written in bold, cursive letters with flowers all around. And then the third frame would have them asking, "Well why don't you just leave that Buck for this Donnie Sessions boy?" And I would list the reasons why, one frame after the next. And each frame would get sillier. The fourth frame: because Donnie lives in one of those old Airstreams. It is really cute. However, I want me a house with big glass doors that slide open onto a sundeck. The fifth frame: he has a rock and roll poster on every wall except for his bathroom, which is wallpapered in *Playboy* bunny foldouts. Not exactly your good environment for children. The sixth frame: even though he has a job, it is a job selling Plumb Good Hot Dogs. And he drives a car shaped just like a foot-long hot dog, up to and including the little tasseled thing at the end of the wiener which dangles over the license plate that reads #1 HOTDOG. On the sides of the car are such things as: KING OF THE DOUBLE DOG and PLUMB GOOD HOT DOGS, JUST ASK GEORGE PLUMB. And every morning Donnie puts on a little white butcher uniform with a small black bow tie and gets in that thing and rides around town distributing. He loves doing it and has no intention of ever getting a better job.

But he kissed like heaven, so I could overlook some of these faults for the time being. The kissing, of course, is where the comic strip would end.

Now, some smarty pants might come along and ask me why I thought Buck should marry me if I was screwing out on him? My answer would be, there are two sides to every story. My side was that Buck had become disinterested in just about anything that had to do with kissing me. About the most he ever did anymore, besides a rare breakdown, was to come into my room and muss my hair good morning. I could grab him to come to bed but he'd sit on the edge as if Armageddon was right around the corner ready to pounce on him like a rabid dog.

But since that first lost weekend with Donnie, and in a very weak moment, I had made one vow to myself about Buck. I had decided that there would be no more going all the way for Dixie Riggs with any other man until I was out of Buck's house for good.

So Donnie and I sat out on his cement steps sharing two bottles of wine, with me swatting away the mosquitoes and Donnie's hand. But sometimes he would sneak a feel of my breast in such a way that would make it hard put for me to say no. But I did, and under the yellow 40 watt bug light I drove him up the wall until four A.M. at which time I promptly went home to sleep it all off.

Only when I got there, Buck was out in the front yard lifting weights. This is not unusual for Buck. He will follow the schedule I have made for him for training for Mr. Universe even if he is off-schedule and it is four A.M. in the morning. And out under that streetlight, under that moonlight, his shiny tight shorts looked even tighter, even shorter.

"Hello stranger," he said to me.

And I said, "Hello yourself," and stared him up and down. Another thing about Buck, even that late at night he is always perfectly manicured: his hair, his nails, his feet. Even that late at night, he still never picked up a hint dropped. With Buck, I always just had to give it to him straight. So I said, "Oh baby, you sure do look fine. Why don't we go on inside?"

He looked at me blankly and then like any human man, finally gave in. He said, "Oh yeah, well, come on then." With Buck and me, words never have meant a whole lot. I like to think we live on love.

Once inside, I made him close his eyes so I could take off the little leopard lingerie outfit I was wearing. Then I hid it in my pocketbook. He would have been furious if he'd have seen me with something like that. And then, then I kissed Buck's whole perfect body, all the way down to his toes and up again. And when I was finished, he pounced on me like the Bengal tiger on the jungle throw that covered us as he rode me into the strong arms of love. And after what seemed like hours, we kicked off the blanket and he bit my ear. His breath smelled like bananas, his hair, like the history of little boys. He grabbed my hair and jerked me back, kissing the side of my face. Then he turned me over onto my back without leaving me once, kissing me, kissing me, again and again and again. I felt like I was going to fall off a cliff and spiral down through centuries of clouds, with Buck biting my teeth with his, and holding them, holding them, and me, going, going, gone.

And then we were laying back, just breathing, not moving. Of course the truth of the matter was, Buck hadn't moved much at all. He'd just done the usual getting-it-over-with kind of loving. He is not much in bed, I can tell you that much, which is why it is just fortunate for me that he's as good looking as he is. When a man is as good looking as Buck, with all his gorgeous curly brown hair, a woman will dream up practically anything to make him come alive in bed. I almost had myself believing that he really had taken me all those places as I clamped the jungle throw that had never left our bodies up tighter around my neck as he lay on top of me, taking away all my air with his Mr. Universe body.

Suddenly he jumped up and grabbed my hand, dragging me off the bed and onto my knees as we went off into his strange idea of afterplay: prayer. Now don't go getting me wrong. I like to pray with the best of them. But there are just times and places for everything. This never did seem like the time or place to me. But Buck can't stand sinning. So there we were. Me soaked with the sweat of love and Buck soaked with the sweat of sin fear, both of us naked. And who walks through Buck's curtain, but Buck's momma. Now this is something new. This is something to sweat about. She says, "Oh Dixie, I just came to remind you that tomorrow is the day you get baptized."

I said, "Oh Lord, I better buy me some hose," because it was all I could think of to say.

She said, "I've got a brand new pair you can have." Then

she walked out, back into that little insomniac world of hers that she enters every morning around five. Sometimes I've heard her just walk back and forth, back and forth, up and down the hall for hours on end. If ever anyone was meant to be a ghost, it would be Momma Speed.

Buck didn't say a word after she left. He just squeezed my hand tighter and prayed some more. I kept peeking up at Paulette's photograph, wondering if she used to do this same praying thing. And I wondered if she had ever loved Buck enough to turn into a Baptist for him. And I wondered if my Methodist grandmother was rolling over in her grave knowing I was about to.

Finally, when he was finished, Buck helped me off my knees and said, "Momma gets those things at a discount factory through the mail."

"What things?"

"Panty hose."

I am not afraid to tell you that I was still a little embarrassed and shaking like a leaf when I grabbed up my clothes and stumbled out of his room so fast that I didn't even see the china cabinet in the dark. The next thing I knew, I had run into one of its glass doors and the thing exploded! And there I was, sprawled across the shattered plates of fine bone china that lay beneath me, trying to figure out how in the hell Buck knew so much about where his momma bought her hose, when his daddy, of all people, came running in to see what the commotion was about. I, of course, being stark naked. I could see the last gleam of Dixie Riggs leave from his solid Christian eyes right then and there. From that time on I knew I would be right up there on the top of his list with Sparkle's cousin, Leslie-Lester.

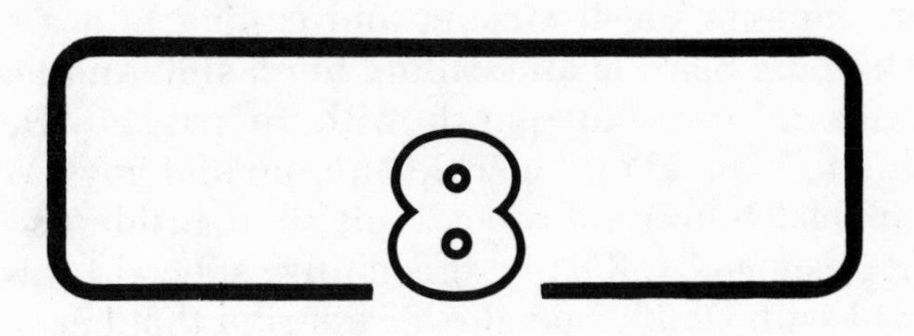

I can tell immediately that Sparkle has had a go of the wrong thing when she shows up on the Speeds' doorstep at seven o'clock the next morning, her eyes all swollen red from crying. Everyone was getting ready for church, for my baptism. Buck was doing some early morning bodybuilding in his room. Momma Speed had bacon cooking crisp in the skillet. Daddy Speed was doing what he always did on Sunday mornings, listening to the gospel station as he put on his suit and tie.

I pushed Sparkle out on the front lawn and said, "Okay kid, let's hear it."

Immediately I can tell I am not ready for this. She says, "Momma caught me sitting half naked next to her boyfriend and she kicked me out of her house. You should have seen her face. This time it's for good, Dixie."

She said this as if it wasn't the first time it had happened between her and Trina. I had to think hard about this scene in order to get the full impact, for only the full impact would move me to help her out. For one thing, because I know Sparkle well enough to know that what her momma saw was not Sparkle sitting half naked next to that man, but sitting completely naked and on him. Kissing all up on his face, making Trina the last thing on his mind. Sparkle does not have a loyal bone in her body when it comes to men.

She started explaining the whole thing to me: about her mother slapping the boyfriend and calling him a bastard. Then slapping Sparkle and calling her a slut. And I couldn't help but to think about Sparkle with my past boyfriends.

Let me tell you about Sparkle and me and boys. We have these special homing devices built right inside us just for men. Me especially. It's like this nature special I saw on TV one night with Daddy Speed where it said that bees only fill up with enough fuel to take them to their honey source. They must find it or else they won't have enough fuel to take them back home. That'll be it for their little bee lives. Well it's that way with me and boys. I fill up on one guy and always make sure there's another one to go to before I let go of the one I have, or else I go crazy. I have to have a man. Now I finally understand what the phrase "the birds and the bees" means. It never really made a whole lot of sense to me before. It was always kind of like the saying "you can have your cake and eat it too," which still doesn't make a whole lot of sense if you ask me.

Anyway I swear I'm exactly like a bee. They can only see certain colors. They are color blind to others. It's like that with me and men too. I won't go with just anybody. No. I like a dark-haired man with big strong shoulders, a big nose, green eyes and dimples, like Buck. I will also go for blonds and bald men, but I have a hard time seeing a redheaded man. They can be cute as the devil but my eyes just glaze over when I see one.

Another strange thing about bees. The bee will scout out a place where the nectar is, then come back to the hive and do a little dance telling exactly where and how far away it is. It's that way with me and Sparkle. I'm like the scout. I tell her what the man's like in bed, how much money he has, what kind of car he drives, and she goes out and gets him. I have never had a problem with this. It has actually been very good for everyone involved. Number one: I have fun with a man. Number two: Sparkle takes my place and has fun with him. Number three: He begins to have fun with Sparkle, thereby keeping his mooning for me down to a minimum. So far it has worked out beautifully.

There is only one man I would not accept this with and that is my Buck. But as I said before, Buck and Sparkle hate the living daylights out of each other, so it is not something I'm going to have to worry about. Just like I know that the next time I will have to put another quart of oil in my old Dodge Charger again before I drive away, I know Sparkle wouldn't be caught dead in the fresh air with Buck, much less his bedroom. And Buck wouldn't touch Sparkle even if she was on her bended knee pleading for him to.

But here she was asking me for help and so I did the only other stupid thing I could think of. I took her in the kitchen and sat her down at the table, and turned the bacon for Momma Speed so she could change. Then I picked up the phone to call Donnie Sessions, getting him out of bed.

He said, "Ohhh Dixie, baby, you are all I ever think about."

"Well listen here, Donnie. I need a big favor."

And I could tell immediately that he had rolled over on his back and was doing that certain thing that I guess all men do in the morning. He breathed heavy and said, "Anything baby. Anything at all."

And then Buck walked into the kitchen wearing this nice linen suit, took one look at Sparkle and turned right back around and walked out, and I said to Donnie, "Well listen here hon, I can't talk just yet, but do you think you could put my friend Sparkle up for a few days?"

He said, "Dixie, I could put up the Empire State Building for you." Well, I wasn't about to get into *that* because I heard his sheets rustling in such a way that I knew I was being set up for some kind of slimy talk so I just said, "Well thank you very much. I'll send her right on over," and hung up.

Sparkle immediately started in with, "Oh Dixie, I don't even know this guy. Couldn't you go with me?"

I said, "Sparkle, when has this ever been a problem for you? Listen, get a move on. I've got to get ready for church. Besides, Buck can't stand you being here. Listen, Donnie says it's okay for a few days. You think you can get things worked out with Trina by then?"

She said, "I doubt it, Dixie. She was pretty pissed off. But maybe me and Donnie could get a little something going, huh?" She took a piece of bacon and ate around the corners, grinning.

Yep, it would be a long time before her mother let her back in that house. "Sparkle, keep your hands off Donnie. Right now he's mine."

"Oh Dixie," she said, pretending to pout. "Haven't you ever heard of sharing?"

I knew her so well. "All right, Sparkle. Cut it out. You want a place to stay or not?"

She quit grinning. "Dixie, you don't have to worry about me. Do I look like I'm in a position to cause any more trouble?"

She had a point, but with Sparkle you can never tell.

The next hour found me at the Ocean Highway Baptist Church. Not one person in Buck's family said a word, not a hint, about the night before. The china had been cleaned up and cleared out. Buck's daddy still wasn't speaking to me but Buck's momma helped me to get dressed. She put me in her finest church skirt and blouse and shoes. I spent an entire hour getting my hair ready. When we arrived at the church, Miss Branch, the church secretary who is reedy and thin and looks just like a branch herself, took me behind the pulpit and told me that I would probably like to take my clothes off before I put on my white baptismal gown.

"You'll be wanting something dry to wear after being dunked." She said this as she carefully hung the glossy robe up, smoothing it out. "Just leave on your bra and panties and you'll be just fine."

I hadn't worn a bra or panties. All I had on was a pair of Momma Speed's Underalls hosiery, the kind with the panties built in. So just as soon as Miss Branch left, I took off everything including them. Nothing is worse than a pair of wet panty hose. Then I slipped the beautiful white robe carefully over my styled hair and waited.

I could hear everything from behind the pulpit. The choir

broke into a verse of "Have Thine Own Way" and in that back room, all alone, I quietly sang along:

Have Thine own way, Lord,
Have Thine own way.
Thou art the potter,
I am the clay.
Mold me and make me
After Thy will,
While I am waiting
yielded and still.

My voice broke when I tried to hit the high notes, and even though nobody else was in the room, I looked around embarrassed and sat down. But then I stood right back up. I didn't want to wrinkle the white robe. Instead, I walked around in circles while the preacher said a few prayers for the newly departed and the loved ones who were too ill to make it to the service. It was a long list, starting with Mr. Jerome Branch, Miss Branch's uncle, who had been on the list for years, ever since he had stopped coming to church. So said Daddy Speed. There were prayers for Mike Byrd, who had the flu, and Shirley Campbell because she'd just lost her husband to an illness, although everyone knew what it really was, was that he'd run off to Texas with his secretary. The list went on and on, finally ending with dear old Mrs. Connie Zuckerman who was still in the hospital with kidney failure. She was the only one I really knew, besides the Speeds, and I missed seeing her on Sundays. She always wore the cutest little hats.

After the prayers, the preacher went straight into one of his long sermons. So I read the titles of the books on the shelves. They were such that I felt my heart drop. All the books were on marriage: *Love and Marriage. Sanctifying the Holy Bonds of Matrimony. Marriage in the Church.* Lord! Here I was, about to get baptized, and everybody in this small little marriage-minded church was going to be watching. Whenever me and Buck had walked down that church aisle these past Sundays, not one person had been left with the illusion that Buck Speed was ever going to marry me. Even Buck's momma had taken to sitting in the balcony far away from us because, she said, she couldn't stand the way Miss Branch sung. But I knew why. Just like I knew why, except for today, Buck's daddy came to the earlier services. They were ashamed of me. And where the congregation used to welcome me with open arms, now every Sunday they just turned their heads to the stained glass windows and watched the crippled men at Christ's feet as I walked by. They couldn't stand to look at me. They acted like I was the crippled one, with both of my legs chopped off, a hump on my back and wasn't that a shame. I pictured them coming up the aisle to shake my hand and kiss my cheek and hug me after the baptismal service, and then turning away to whisper to their husbands, "Ahh, that Dixie Riggs. I hope this takes. I hope she can remain a good Christian woman, what with her living in sin the way she does."

I shuddered. Reading the titles of those books about marriage made me so weak that I felt like running out the back door. And I was just about to but one of the deacons came in the room and grabbed me and hugged me all up and told me, "You are one lucky woman today, getting saved for the Lord." Then he led me down a small hallway, where a young boy with a closely shaved head was standing with his back to us. In front of the young boy stood the preacher in chest high water, still preaching his mighty storm of a sermon.

The preacher was the Honorable Reverend Doctor Wayne Whatley, holding a leather Bible that drooped over either side of his hand as if it were an elephant's ear. A red marker fell from Galatians and trailed the tip of the water. He read, the choir sang, everyone prayed. I tried to bow my head to pray but I couldn't help looking up at the flashing red light that was above the water. First it flashed red and then it flashed yellow and then it was flashing green, flashing like a traffic light, flashing for the little boy in front of me to lead his old sinning life into the new cleansing one of the baptismal pool.

Reverend Whatley held his hand out to the boy and guided him down the steps into the water to join him. I moved forward. A cold draft ran up my legs. With nothing on underneath, it cooled off the nervous part of me. It made me feel calmer. It made me feel good. It made me think about Buck and Donnie and all the other boys. But then I heard Preacher Whatley talking about Jesus and I told myself that I'd better not be thinking about boys, that I'd better be thinking about Jesus. I started repeating "Jesus, Jesus" inside my head, craning my neck to see if I could catch a glimpse of Momma Speed. If I could only see her face, I'd remember the grace of Jesus. But all I could see was Miss Branch's head as it bobbed up and down as she said her amens to Preacher Whatley's spoken word.

Suddenly it came to me. It bolted up my spine like I'd been struck by cold lightning. Once my robe got wet all my naked parts would show through. I should have worn a bra. I should have worn panties. Preacher Whatley droned on. He read a long passage from Corinthians. I was getting itchy all over. When he began a chapter in Thessalonians, I started for the back. I just had to put my hose back on. But the deacon grabbed my arm and whispered, "Don't worry. Everyone's nervous when they do this." He smiled and pressed a firm hand on me just like the preacher kept his hand firm on the small boy's head.

The boy squirmed. He was so young, I wondered if he even knew what he was doing up there. If he was saying "Jesus, Jesus" inside his head like I was, believing it to be true, or if his momma and daddy had said, "Well, he's twelve years old now," and made him come. He stretched his left foot out as far as he could, stretching to reach for a quarter that was at the bottom of the tank.

The preacher shut the Bible and held it to his chest. Then he dunked the boy. The boy still tried for the quarter while Preacher Whatley held him under. But then the light turned green again, and the preacher pulled him up and guided him out the other side of the pool and suddenly it was my turn.

The deacon gently nudged me to go ahead. I held back. I felt so naked under my robe. My small breasts felt like huge jiggling water balloons ready to burst. I couldn't do it. I just couldn't do it. But then the deacon pushed me forward and Preacher Whatley reached his giant hand out for mine, a hand wide enough to hold a basketball, and slowly he pulled me down the stairs into the water. I tried to fold the robe in front of me the best way I could, but it ballooned up around me like a parachute.

I pushed it down frantically with my free hand while Reverend Whatley pressed on my head with his big hand and read from Corinthians loudly. It felt like he was shouting in my ear. It felt like my nipples were standing at attention. I held the cloth firm around my legs. Finally, after what seemed like forever, he dunked me. I didn't have a chance to get air. I swallowed water. I saw my own bubbles dancing down to the quarter the boy hadn't got, then back up around Preacher Whatley's floating pants legs. My gown billowed up again. It swirled up and up, all around me like a white day lily. I was so embarrassed. I kept thinking to myself, "Jesus, Jesus, please keep me covered," and then it was over. I walked up the stairs, out of the pool, with my gown clinging to me like wet toilet paper.

I rushed back and changed into my dry Sunday clothes. My hair, which before had spent an hour in hot rollers, was sopping wet when I walked back out to stand in front of the congregation for the closing prayer. It felt good to be dressed. After we all sang the Benediction, the church members came up and shook our hands just like I knew they would. The young boy stood next to me in a tie that was too big, shuffling back and forth from one foot to the other. His hair was so short, it wasn't even wet anymore.

I knew that now Buck Speed would never marry me. In the back of my mind I had hoped all along that if I turned into a Baptist, God would smile on me and let me be Buck's wife. But that hope was gone now. I had done the worst thing. I had embarrassed Buck Speed in front of the whole church.

I saw him and his momma making their way to me. They were going to walk right past me without saying a word and shake the boy's hand and get out of there fast. I could see it in their faces. They were furious. Momma Speed's face was scrunched up like if she'd had a gun she'd have shot me clean through the head with it.

Then Buck was by my side. He was beaming. His arm was around me. I couldn't believe it. And Momma Speed was there too, crying and kissing me and saying, "I am so happy. You looked so pretty up there." Then everyone was shaking my hand and kissing me and saying, "Didn't she look pretty though. Now wasn't she a pretty thing. She looked like she had been kissed by the angels."

Even Miss Branch stuck her hand out and said, "You were very beautiful up there, Dixie Riggs. This is the most important day of your Christian life . . ." which trailed off into the memory of the first time I had decided to get baptized. I remembered clearly because that was back when Buck and me were first in love, and he was loving me all day long. It had been the third time I had gone to their church that the Holy Spirit had come up on me. When the preacher had called out for any lost souls, I had walked up to the pulpit proudly.

I looked at Buck now, all manicured in his perfect off-white linen suit with his snazzy shoes, the same Buck that had beamed at me when I had first answered that call, and my strength vanished. What if I'd just accepted God for all the wrong reasons? What if, because I had made my vows to get Buck, I would lose Buck forever? Visions of other women being dunked for the wrong reasons swam around inside my wet head. Dunked and abandoned, I envisioned them walking the streets of small towns with suitcases in their hands, nowhere to go, no one to take them in. And worse, with God's unmerciful wrath upon them.

Buck's momma took me by the arm and hugged me one more time. "Dixie," she said, "I am so proud of you, I could cry." And she did, crying the horrible visions away.

She led me out the church door. I shook Miss Branch's hand once more, hugged Shirley Campbell, the one who had lost her husband, and then I shook Preacher Whatley's hand. He said, "Tough time with that robe, huh?" and winked at me. I turned beet red, and Momma Speed hugged me again. Then me and her turned to follow Buck, who still didn't have a wrinkle in his suit, and who walked two feet ahead of us, just like Prince Charles does with Princess Diana. And I thought, I could learn to love walking two feet behind my Buck, because after all, I was more in love with Buck Speed at that moment than I had ever been with anyone in my entire life.

Dixie, how about you go fixing us a little something to eat and we'll watch us some TV," is the first thing Buck said to me when we got back from church. He wrapped his arm around my shoulders and squeezed me. And let me tell you, it felt right. It felt domestic. It felt like something was about to happen. I went into the kitchen, where Momma Speed was fixing Daddy Speed some lunch, and worked around her. She hugged me again, too, and said, "Dixie, this is the most important day of your life. Why don't you sit down and I'll make some dinner for the both of you?"

So I said, "No thank you, ma'am. But listen," I whispered. "I feel like maybe this is the turning point for Buck and me, if you know what I mean." I winked at her and held my hand up in the air as if to examine an invisible engagement ring. "I want to make sure I'm doing my part, if you know what I mean."

It took Momma Speed a minute, but then she was hugging me and swinging me all around the kitchen and we were squealing together, future momma-in-law, future daughter-in-law.

"Shh, shh!" I said. "I don't want Buck to hear us. I want him to think he's surprising me."

"Dixie, I can't believe it," she whispered, about to burst

screaming, holding me away from her so she could get a good look at me. "He asked you?! He finally asked you?! I just know I'm going to die right here on the spot from happiness. Finally, a daughter!"

I whispered, "Hold your horses, Momma Speed. He hadn't asked me yet. But I just know he's going to. It's just something that tells me so. I can't explain it, but you can bet you that before the hour's up, I'll be back in here with some news that will send both of our heads reeling."

She squeezed me again. "Oh, I will love for you to be my daughter!"

For the next ten minutes we were grinning like old fools, not saying a word, while I fixed Buck a BLT and a cheese omelet, two very nutritious and protein-filled foods guaranteed to give a Mr. Universe the energy he needs to train. And Buck had to get busy training harder. I would see to that. I was determined to be the best wife a man could have. The kind of wife where everyone would say to Buck, "That little woman of yours is a real catch, a real jewel. You really hit the jackpot when you met her, mister."

While I put the finishing touches on the omelet, an extra shot of Velveeta and a parsley sprig, Momma Speed brought me a TV dinner tray. Then she went into the china cabinet and pulled out a few good plates, ones that I had not broken the night before. She surrounded them with some of the sterling silverware that she never even took out for company unless of course it was Preacher Whatley visiting. To top it off, she added a fine linen napkin and some azaleas from her garden. Then it was time to carry the tray to Buck. Momma Speed kissed me on the cheek and I was on my way, through the curtain, past Buck's bed and past Paulette who still smiled over Buck's bed like she knew nobody could ever take her place in his heart. I stuck my tongue out at her and thought, "You will be the FIRST thing to go."

Buck, being a man, did not even take notice of the elaborate meal I set up for him in front of his big wide-screen TV. But that is okay, for like I said, he is a man and a man will not do that. So then I loved him even more because I could understand his flaws and overlook them. I could see it now. I'd be fixing him all the little things he loved so much and he wouldn't have a clue. He'd just sit there and eat them as if I'd slapped together a peanut butter sandwich, and when Sparkle came over, and my other friends too, they'd say, "How can you stand him? Doesn't it bother you? Look at all you do for him and he doesn't even give you the time of day." I'd just throw back my head and laugh and say, "Oh boys will be boys. Come on girls, I'll make us some coffee," and they'd all die with jealousy that me and Buck had the perfect marriage.

I watched with pride as he ate and watched TV. "The 700 Club" was on. It was his favorite show.

"Now see him, Dixie," said Buck, pointing to a televangelist who wore three diamond rings on one hand. "That is what I call a good preacher. See how he works his audience? You can tell by the way he spreads his hands in the air that he means what he says."

I didn't know about that. I did, however, know for a fact, thanks to Sparkle who teaches me everything about hair, that he used Grecian Formula to get that awful brown hair color of his, and that he left the sides gray on purpose for effect. That was not the kind of look I'd trust in a man. It was an adultery-thieving kind of look to me.

"Now watch this," Buck said. "Watch how he wraps this up."

Ten clean white phones were ringing behind the televangelist and ten clean girls were picking them up. The small choir that sang behind him swayed left, then right. He closed his Bible slowly and brought it around to press at his lower back. And there, holding it tight, he told the story of Jesus on the cross.

I cut my eyes to watch Buck. He was mesmerized. His hands were clutching his knees. Every one of his fingernails were shaped as perfect as the next. Every one of those fingernails was going to be mine. He picked up his sandwich and never dropped a crumb. Me, I would have had crumbs all over my lap. Everything I did, he did better, and that was just fine, since everything he did was going to belong to me, Mrs. Buck Speed the Third.

A commercial came on featuring Efrem Zimbalist, Jr.,

reading from the complete unedited edition of *The Living Bible* on cassette tapes for only forty-nine dollars and ninety-five cents, all major credit cards accepted. And that's when Buck turned to me. He said, "You know, Dixie, I was watching you up there today and it came to me that maybe we should go on ahead and tie the knot."

I cringed at "tie the knot," but then I quickly remembered that it was a good thing to love his flaws. I could laugh about it later to him, to our children, to our grandchildren. I'd say, "And then he said, and get this, he said, 'How about we tie the knot?' "

I tried to look Buck in the eye, but he wouldn't look at me, so I said, "Are you sure, honey?"

He said, "Well, do you think you'd mind living with Momma for a while?"

"Oh Buck, I couldn't think of a thing I'd like more."

"And baby I want you to forget what I said about you paying rent. You don't need no job. No wife of mine is ever going to work."

Well, we'd talk about that later. Nothing was going to get in my way of being a big time model now. Nothing short of what Paulette was would be good enough for me. It came to me that I should ask him to take her picture down, but I decided not to push things.

And he said, "Oh, now watch this," talking about "The 700 Club" again. "Watch how he starts the next part of the show by going up to one person in the audience and directing the sermon at them. That is real art, Dixie, a real personal touch."

I did not know about it being a personal touch or a real art, except maybe being an art to take somebody's money, but I did know that I could not wait to tell Momma Speed, who I knew would be sitting on the sofa cross-stitching, just about dying to hear the news. I knew she'd be the one to pick out the date and it would be the fastest one she could get. I knew she'd call Preacher Whatley and remind him that even though it was June and the church was booked up, she'd been coming to his church since she was a little girl, longer than he'd preached there for that matter, and she'd never once asked a favor but did he think . . . ? That's what I knew.

Buck quickly grabbed my hand and said, "Give me a kiss, girl." So I did. Our first kiss as an engaged couple.

"Dixie," he said, "I'm going to be as good as he is about getting the Word around."

The preacher on "The 700 Club" got a round of applause. Buck threw his head back and looked to the ceiling. He was so pleased with the TV preacher. He looked so contented. I wanted to always watch my Buck watch TV. I was so happy. Now I know this all sounds so stupid, but when you look right into the very heart of it, love is not saying anything bad about his heroes even when you know they're down to the core rotten. It means loving his perfect fingernails even when you wish maybe just this once he'd break down and get them a little dirty.

I could have sat there for days, not eating, just breathing it all in. But Buck's daddy called from the kitchen.

"What is it, Daddy?" asked Buck.

"Come here, son," he said. I could tell he was standing by the refrigerator, just staring at the door like he always did.

"We're busy, Daddy. Come on in here."

"No, I think you'd better come in here, son."

"What is it with that man?" asked Buck, irritated. "Hold on, Dixie, I'll be right back."

But I knew what it was. I knew that Buck's daddy still hated me. He wanted me gone. He wouldn't even speak to me anymore unless he had to, unless Momma Speed told him to. He hadn't even hugged me at church. He'd just walked by and nodded and walked out the door. He was going to be a problem, but a problem that could be overcome. I had faith in my Buck that he would take care of all the problems of our home.

The plants in Buck's room rustled, as a hot, sticky summer breeze blew in through the window. I brushed the crumbs from his plate into his favorite schefflera plant. From now on I wouldn't only feed Buck, I would make up special foods for his plants. Of course, I'd have to find room in my busy modeling schedule to do it, but I would mark a little place in our new refrigerator that read "Buck's Plants." Maybe I'd make a little health-snack shelf, too, labeled Monday, Tuesday, Wednesday, Thursday and so forth, so that while Buck trained for the Mr. Universe Contest, he would be able to eat a balanced diet of snacks whenever he wanted, even if I was off at the mall with the girls.

It was hard to believe that me, Dixie Riggs, from Cordele, Georgia, was finally going to turn into Dixie Speed, from Myrtle Beach, South Carolina, home of the Grand Strand. I couldn't wait to have a bunch of little Myrtle Beach High School quarterbacks running around our house. Like Buck who used to be quarterback at the Myrtle Beach High School. Now he was standing over me, holding a brown envelope in his hand. And he was furious.

It was addressed to Mr. Buck Speed, Jr. That was Buck's daddy's name. Buck was Buck Speed the Third. I took the envelope and opened it the wrong way and all the naked photographs of myself wearing the nippleless bra, and myself wearing the leopard panties, and myself wearing this and that and nothing at all, went spilling to the floor. I didn't know what to say. But Buck did. He said, "Dixie Riggs, Daddy said this package was laying against the door this morning. I don't guess you've got a thing to say, do you?"

I shook my head, amazed.

"Well then, I think maybe it's time you leave."

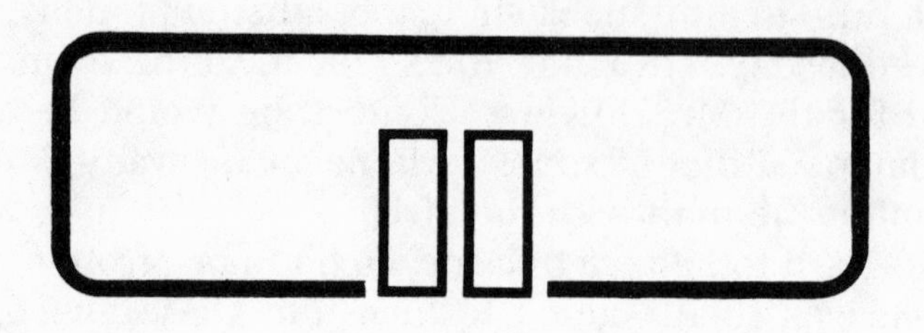

I said nothing. For the first time since I was born I had nothing to say. "The 700 Club" was praying for Mrs. Aboline Montgomery of Oak Ridge, Tennessee, who was recovering from a liver operation, and I couldn't say a thing. I picked up the pictures, which were suspiciously void of Sparkle. I just didn't know what to do. There just wasn't anything I could do.

I walked past the knowing Paulette, to the den where Momma Speed was sitting, cross-stitching like I knew she'd be. It was a new pattern with Buck's and my name written out in pencil over our engagement date, ready to be stitched, and I did exactly as I had promised before. I told her news that would send us both reeling. That Mr. Speed and Buck were going to help the newly baptized porno queen quietly pack, then load up her car, which they did, and without saying a word. I was so embarrassed. I remembered thinking that very morning that something bad like this was going to happen. A woman just cannot get baptized for the wrong reasons. I kept repeating in my head, over and over again, "I am sorry Jesus, I am sorry Jesus, please Jesus, don't let this be happening. I'll go right on back and do it the right way. I am sorry Jesus. Please, please, please, please, please, please, please." But no lightning bolt struck out of the sky and turned back the clock of time. As soon as the car was packed Mr. Speed left Buck and me all alone.

Buck said, "Now Dixie, I love you girl. You know I love you. But my daddy's just too hurt by this and he thinks it'd be better if we didn't see each other for a while. Here," he said, pulling three crisp one-hundred-dollar bills from his wallet. "I was saving this up for when we got married. You're going to need to take it. I've kept you from working and you're going to need something to live on. We'll get you an apartment today and then let a little time go by and then we'll see, okay?"

"We'll see" meant "I, Buck Speed the Third, will never marry a tramp like Dixie Riggs the porno queen." I could see it in his eyes, feel it in his cold body next to mine as he stiffened up like a rod, and hugged me good-bye with one arm.

I said, "Now you listen here, Mr. Buck Speed. I don't need your help for nothing. You understand that? I can find my own way, thank you very much." I threw the money at his feet. I got in my car. I slammed the door. I couldn't see out the back for all the packing. I couldn't see anything for crying so hard. I reached over and patted around for the one thing I could get a little comfort from. I felt around for the picture of Paulette that I'd taken. It was there, all right, just where I'd put it. If Buck Speed wasn't going to be thinking about me anymore, he damn well wasn't going to be thinking about Miss Pan Am Paulette. I put the car in reverse, stripping the gears, and squealed out the driveway. My whole life had slowed, stopped and started backing up and was now in full reverse going out of Buck's life.

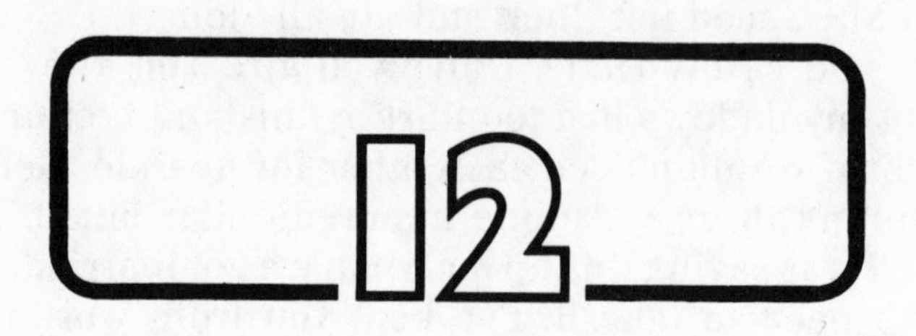

I went to find Sparkle. I could see that much. It didn't take a genius to see that much. I gunned the engine all the way to Donnie's Airstream, where his lawn was brown and his hot dog car was parked right out front.

Donnie opened the door and came outside. "What's up Dixie?"

I screamed, "Where's that bitch?!"

He said, "Sparkle?"

I screamed, "Yes, Sparkle. Of course, Sparkle."

He said, "Come here, baby. Sit down and tell me what's wrong. You look all upset."

I jerked his hand away. "Where the hell is she?!"

"Okay, okay. Don't go getting all touchy, babe. She's inside taking a nap."

She was in the trailer, all right, sleeping on the couch. I jerked her up and slapped her as hard as I could and then I started tearing her hair out.

"Stop Dixie! Stop! What the hell are you doing?!" she screamed, holding the roots of her hair.

"Why'd you do it?" I yelled, jerking her head back farther, spitting at her when I spoke.

"What Dixie, do what?" she cried. "Let go of me!"

I jerked her back once more, then pushed her across the

room onto the floor. Then I jumped on top of her and started hitting her again and again and again. "Okay you little snot-nosed bitch. Spill it. I want to know *why*!"

Donnie ran back and tried to pull me off her, but I turned around to him and said, "If you ever, *ever*, want to sleep with me again, then you'd better get the hell out of here and I mean *now*!"

He stood up and went to stand by the door.

"I don't know what you're talking about," screamed Sparkle.

"Oh come off it," I said. "The pictures, Miss Priss. Remember the pictures?"

"What pictures?"

"Don't give me that crap, you little bitch." I grabbed her hair again. "You know good and well what pictures. The *naked* pictures!" I yelled. "You were the only one who had them." I grabbed a thick glass ashtray from Donnie's coffee table and held it up to hit her.

"No Dixie, don't!" yelled Donnie. He rushed over and grabbed my arm.

"Listen to me," said Sparkle. She was holding her hands high in the air to guard herself. "I don't know what you're talking about. I swear. Did someone get hold of the pictures?"

"Try Buck," I said. I still wanted to hit her with the ashtray, but suddenly she went limp.

"Buck? Oh shit," she said. "Buck got the pictures of us?"

"Look," said Donnie, loosening his grip on me. "I don't know what yall are talking about, but if I were you, I'd put the ashtray down now, Dixie."

I let the ashtray drop. Me and Sparkle just sat there as it thumped down and rolled around on the linoleum floor. Finally I said, "Well, if you didn't send them, who did? Now there's a good question. Answer me that one, huh?"

Sparkle rubbed her head where I'd hit her. "I don't know. I guess whoever developed them. Momma's boyfriend, maybe? I don't know. I ran out of there so fast, I must've left them at his apartment."

"Oh, right," I said.

She said, "No. It had to have been Momma. She must've done it. She was mad enough, that's for sure."

I got up and sat on the couch, my head in my hands. Sparkle didn't move from where she was. No one spoke. I thought about Buck staring at the pictures. Pictures of me wearing that ridiculous tasseled thing. I thought about Daddy Speed seeing the ones of me sitting on Sparkle's lap, naked. Oooooh, the horror! Then it flashed at me again. None of those pictures had Sparkle in them. They were just naked pictures of me. I flew at Sparkle again.

"All right you little sleaze bitch, cough it up!" I yelled, yanking her hair back with one hand, choking her with the other. "Why'd you do it?"

"Stop Dixie! You're hurting me!"

"Ha!" I choked her harder, pulled her hair so hard that I could hear it tearing. "Hurting you? Poor baby. I'll show you what hurting you is all about." I let her go and started kicking her. "It's one thing to screw me over like that, but then to lie to me like I'm some sort of fool. You weren't even in those pictures you slimy little bitch."

"Stop Dixie! Stop! I swear, I don't know why. Stop! Please! You're hurrrrrting me!"

Donnie ran back over and pulled me off her. "Hold up, girl. Hold up."

I kicked Sparkle one more time, hard, before I fell back on the couch to wait. I didn't know what I was waiting for. More energy maybe, because I was planning on beating the shit out of Sparkle the minute Donnie was gone.

But he wasn't going anywhere. "Would yall mind telling me what's going on here?" he said.

I gave Sparkle the evil eye. "Okay. Here's the deal. We made these nudie pictures together, see, and she sent them to Buck, see. But here's the catch. She left the ones of herself out of the package, see. Get the picture now?"

"I did not!" cried Sparkle. "I'm telling you. Momma must've done it."

"What do you think I am? A fool?" I jumped up to beat her up again. But Donnie grabbed me back.

And then Sparkle said, "Look, Dixie. Just think a minute.

Momma would know if she sent them to Buck, he'd get mad at you, then you'd get mad at me and kick me out."

"Dammit," I said, "that doesn't make any sense."

"Oh Dixie, of course it does. She thinks I'm staying with you. And she's so mad at me right now she'd love to see me walking the streets with nowhere to go. Get it?"

I sat down beside her. "All right. Maybe you're right."

Sparkle got on the couch and put her arm around me. She said, "Come on, Dixie. Why else would I be staying in a pigsty like this?"

"Yeah." I laughed. "You've got a point there."

"Thanks a whole hell of a lot, girls," Donnie said, sitting down on the couch between us. He started tickling us both. "But you're wrong. What you see before you is a palace of love."

There wasn't a thing much we could do except hang out at Donnie's. Sparkle didn't have anywhere to go. I didn't have anywhere to go. Donnie couldn't have been happier. He was ready to marry us both for just one night of hot sex.

I wish I had stood up to Buck, lied and said something about my face being superimposed on someone else's body. I could have done it. I'm a good enough liar. But it all happened so fast. I just couldn't even think quick enough.

So there I was, five o'clock Sunday afternoon at Donnie's Airstream trailer trying to throw together dinner out of cans, instead of getting ready for the evening sermon at Buck's church, of which I could not even begin to think about due to the embarrassment of the situation. Instead, I was preparing a meal of Van de Camp's kidney beans and Van de Camp's pork and beans mixed together as the vegetable dish, Franco-American cheese spaghetti as the entree, and shredded lettuce as the salad. We would dine on chinette paper plates with plastic picnic forks. All courtesy of the local minimart where Donnie shops twice a day since he doesn't own a refrigerator. All he owns in the way of appliances are a toaster oven, a two-eye electric range and an ice chest. He didn't have any salad dressing so I stopped crying, which I'd been doing ever since I'd gotten there, and mixed up a half cup of mayonnaise and a half cup of ketchup. It was my mother's recipe and if it was good enough for Momma, it was sure as hell good enough for Donnie Sessions, who sometimes ate right out of the cold can anyway. Donnie is just that way.

I, myself, would like to know if there have ever been any educational TV documentaries done on the average white American male living in Airsteams. I, for one, think the material is all there. The mating ritual is not unlike that of the Yąnomamös, a South American Indian tribe that I learned about while watching TV with Daddy Speed one night. After the men eat, they crawl into the hut of the woman and that is that. He'd been driving me up the wall all day, squeezing my shoulder blades, stroking my hair, rubbing my feet. For the first time since I'd met him I didn't want to have a thing to do with him. I just wanted to eat my food, go to sleep and wake up in someone else's life. It seemed possible too, if I could just sleep. But there would be no sleeping with Donnie Sessions around. Especially after he ate. I thought about starving him.

I said, "Go on, Donnie. Where's Sparkle? Why don't you try Sparkle? That's a good idea. I won't mind a bit. Really."

"Come on, honey. She's all drunk and passed out. Besides, she ain't you, Dixie." He said this while I stirred the beans in his one aluminum pot and the spaghetti in his one frying pan, as he grabbed my breasts for I don't know how many times that day.

"Quit, Donnie," I said, lowering the heat. "I've got to go check on that girl."

I'd felt bad all day for beating her up. I'd torn out her hair. I'd given her a black eye. Now she was curled up on the couch in Donnie's sleeping bag looking like she was twelve. An old rerun of "Wild Kingdom" was on TV. Marlin Perkins was trying to relocate a wild rhino. Marlin Perkins was always relocating something. He could come on and relocate me, is what I thought, as me and Donnie relocated Sparkle into the back room. He had her under the arms, I had her by the feet. She was definitely out for the night and I was jealous.

Donnie and me ate and watched TV with the lights off. I'd turned them off. I hadn't wanted to watch him drop his crumbs. Every few minutes or so he would reach over and put his hand between my legs or on my breast.

"Quit Donnie," I'd say. "I'm trying to watch this."

And he'd say, "Now come on, Dixie. You know you can't do this to me."

And I'd say, "Do what?"

And he'd groan, "Oh come on, Dixie. You know what. You're giving me blue balls."

And I'd say, "That's grossness, Donnie. Pure-T grossness."

And he'd say, "I know, but I can't help it. Please, Dixie, have a heart. How about if you just hold it."

"Leave me alone." It was right about in there that I began to miss Buck more than I could breathe. I looked at Donnie's Miller High Life clock. It was eight o'clock straight up. The Speeds would be walking into their house from church. Momma Speed would say, "Oh my aching feet," pretending like nothing bad had happened all day apart from her shoes.

And Daddy Speed would say, "Hey Momma, you got some of that ice tea in there," and without saying another word he and Buck would go sit in front of Daddy Speed's TV and start fighting over what to watch. The pain of what I'd done shot through my veins like a horrible acid. I was going to bleed. I was going to die from the inside out. All I wanted in the whole wide world was to be sitting between them wishing I wasn't there, instead of not being there at all.

"Come on, Dixie," Donnie said. He put his hand up my shirt and began squeezing.

"Ouch Donnie! Not so hard. I am not a cantaloupe, you know."

And he laughed. "Well no one accused you of being that."

I said, "Oh ha ha."

Donnie said, "Oh baby, you feel so good." He pinched my nipple real soft, just like I liked it. I still missed Buck, but I was beginning to relax. "That's a girl," he said.

Then the phone rang. I shot straight up. "Answer it!" I yelled. "If it's Buck, don't tell him I'm here."

"That's okay, baby. Lay back. There's nobody I need to talk to right now."

"No Donnie. You've got to answer it. It might be Buck!"

"Dixie Riggs, that don't make no sense."

"Donnie, just do it!"

His phone was shaped like a pair of giant lips. I thought I was going to have a heart attack while he tried to dig it out from underneath all his clothes and magazines. Finally he said, "Yup," real irritated. "Donnie here." Then his mood changed. "Well hey bub. What's up?"

"Who is it?" I mouthed. "Buck?"

Donnie brought the phone over to the couch, shaking a pair of dirty jeans off the cord. "Really. Tough break, man."

By this time I'd moved right up on Donnie, trying to listen in. He ran his hand up my shirt again, pulling me close, but still I couldn't hear a thing.

"Who?" I mouthed again, and he winked at me and pulled me in even tighter.

"Well that's a bad break. But it don't sound so bad to me. Dirty pictures don't mean she messed around any. Just sounds like she was having herself a good time," Donnie said, squeezing my boob real hard. "Hey listen, bub, I got someone here just now. How about you and me go to the gym tomorrow and talk it out there? We can figure out what to do then, okay? See ya, bub."

I couldn't believe it. It was Buck. And he was upset over me. He was actually upset over me. He was calling a friend for help. Guilt rushed through me like a forest fire. The sadness was so great I barely had the energy to ward off Donnie's advances. He kept saying, "Come on, Dixie, everything's cool now. He ain't coming over and we've got all night."

But he didn't understand. All I wanted was for my Buck to ride me off into the sunset like a white knight in a good story with a happy ending.

But it was not going to happen. So I began cleaning up the place while Donnie sat on the couch mad as hell that I wouldn't "give him a little bit." He watched Canadian football with his arms folded across his chest and sulked. Well, that's Donnie Sessions for you. In a nutshell.

One thing I don't want to get is bored. I'm not one of those secretary types that have everything in perfect order, who think things through one step at a time and never change their minds, who wear all those little gold chains and sweetheart rings and have cute little dog and cat calendars gracing one wall and a NO SMOKING sign gracing the other. Lord, I don't even *own* a sweetheart ring! If I did, then maybe I wouldn't have gone to bed with Donnie Sessions that night. But I didn't so I did. And I won't say I had a bad time either. One thing about Donnie, he is not a bad time.

It was somewhere around two or three in the morning when I finally finished cleaning up his place, folding all his dirty clothes, all his dirty hot dog uniforms that I swear look a whole lot whiter on than off. He was sacked out on the couch. And Lord! I was starving again. I couldn't face another canned meal and there wasn't anything in his ice chest, so I shook him and said, "Donnie. Wake up, Donnie. Take me to the store."

He reached up and grabbed my breast. "Hmmm?"

"Come on," I said, shaking him harder. "Let's go to the store. I want to go to the store."

So without saying a word he jumped up, zipped his pants

and grabbed his cigarettes. Now let me say one thing here, there is nothing more sexy than a man half asleep.

Since my Charger was still jampacked and it was hard to see out the back window, we crawled into the George Plumb, Plumb Good Hot Dog car. Donnie was too tired to drive so I did the driving while he half slept and half smoked. It was the first time I'd ever driven it. It was skinny and weird, just like you'd imagine.

At the store, I got out and he stayed in, his cigarette ash needing to be flicked. I still had Buck in the back of my mind, but Donnie sitting there in that stupid car with no shirt on was burning a mighty big hole in the front. So I bought two cinnamon rolls, a Dr Pepper, a six-pack of beer and we were back in bed mixing eating and drinking and making love together as if they were all part of the same thing, which that Yąnomamö documentary I'd seen swore was true. It said that the need for sex comes from the same strong need for fulfilling animal hunger that food does.

I could believe it. I was so hungry for Donnie. He was so cute. An old rerun of "Wagon Train" was on TV and the horses were charging and the guns were going off, while he rode me up and moved me out into the sweet wee hours of the night. He kissed my toes, and I liked it. But I could not handle the chills running up and down my spine. So I begged for him to stop which he would not. He tried putting my whole foot in his mouth, and then he bit my legs up, way way up high, and that is not all. And then we were breathing with the rhythm of the galloping horses on "Wagon Train" and then we were spent, as they say. And pretty soon I was lulled into a trance by Donnie's sound-asleep breathing. How does that old saying go? Lying to the one I love, lying next to the one I don't. How strange that the man who could make Roman candles go off in my bed was not the man I wanted to spend the rest of my life with. I was thinking that I'd take my Buck with his dud firecracker self any day over this fiery Donnie Sessions, when all of a sudden there's a wild banging on the window.

"Dixie! Dixie Riggs! You let me in there right now! I know you're in there!"

It was Buck. Buck with a capital B, come to get me and mad as hell. I was not about to open the door. I nudged Donnie but he didn't move. He just whispered, "Shhh," and we laid very still and looked at each other.

Buck was going around the trailer banging on every window. "Dixie, Dixie, you let me in and I mean now!"

I whispered, "Can he see us?"

And Donnie whispered back, "No. There's black paper on the windows."

"Oh yeah. That's right."

We laid there very still, very quiet, very naked, while Buck rattled the front door making the trailer shake. All I could think about was how if I was a Yąnomamö woman, I would not be in this mess, because Yąnomamös do not get married and they do not have cameras. They do not get nudie shots taken of themselves in place of wedding pictures.

I stared at the mobile of *Playboy* bunny pictures that Donnie had above his bed and watched them shake with the trailer. And suddenly the banging stopped. Donnie whispered, "What the fuck's going on now?"

I was afraid to move, even to look at him. I said, "Not sure." I was afraid Buck had woken up Sparkle. I was afraid she would run to the front door and let him in, and he'd find me and Donnie in bed together.

"You think he'll wake up Sparkle?" I whispered, scared.

And he whispered back, "Honey, nothing's going to wake up Sparkle. Stay here."

He got up and lit another cigarette. It seemed like the only noise in the whole world was the whishing of his blue jeans as he slid them on. I watched him tiptoe out the room, down the hall away from me. He was quiet, like a cat.

I got up too and tiptoed to the window. I tried pulling the black paper back but it had been there for too long. The glue had made the glass gooey. And from what little I could see, there was nothing out there anyway.

A hand touched my waist. "What!" I jumped.

And Donnie said, “Shhh, it’s only me. Come here.”

“What is it?” I said.

“Shhh. Just come here.”

I followed him. He opened the venetian blinds on the front door window at a half slant, and then he left me there alone. It was Buck, in running shoes and black satin running shorts, and that was all he had on. He was sitting on the front concrete steps of the Airstream with his back to me. He was flexing and unflexing his muscles, just waiting. Waiting for Dixie Riggs to step foot outside. There wasn’t a sign of his car anywhere. He must have run the four miles over. His back and arms and legs were all oiled and glistening in the trailer park moonlight. I stuck my hand in front of the blind and pressed it lightly against the window, then I walked back to the bed and crawled in, trying not to brush up against Donnie. All of a sudden a fierce tiredness consumed me like fire would someday consume Donnie Sessions’s trailer if he didn’t learn to put out his cigarettes. I rubbed out the burning butt he had left in the ashtray and closed my eyes and thought about how I could walk right out there, right now, and get a big fat marriage proposal out of Buck Speed. I also knew it would end up being me at his house again, wondering when we’d ever get married again, and him not saying again, and his daddy hating me even more. So I had to play this little role out with Donnie Sessions for all it was worth. I had to make sure that when Buck finally did get me back, everyone was going to know it was for good. There wouldn’t be a doubt left in anyone’s mind that I was going to be his wife. But as I said before, right then I was just too tired to even think about it.

15

Well I could tell the part about the next morning when Donnie told Buck this and Buck told Donnie and me that, but I'll just cut through it all and tell the part about what I finally told Buck. I said, "Buck Speed, if you think I slept with Donnie Sessions, you're a sicker man than I thought. Go ahead Donnie, tell him the truth."

Donnie, who had already told him the truth, sucked it back in and told Buck my truth. "I didn't really sleep with her, Buck. We just slept in the same bed." He looked at me as if to ask was that what I wanted, or would I like more of his blood.

I looked hard at him, then at Buck, and said, "See there. Now you ought to be ashamed of yourself. Go on now, Donnie," I said, still looking at Buck. "Me and Buck need to have ourselves a little talk."

It was about eight o'clock the next morning. Buck had spent the entire night sitting on the steps. He had a rough impression of the concrete on the backs of his legs. Donnie, on the other hand, had spent the rest of the night trying to get back in my pants again. I don't know what it is about men, but the minute they sense another man hanging around, their hormones start jumping. Us girls, if we sense another girl hanging around, we put out the DO NOT DISTURB sign on the door. Who can work it out, this thing between men and women?

Anyway, Donnie Sessions wasn't happy. He looked like he felt stupid in his little white butcher uniform telling Buck nothing had happened. And he did look stupid slamming the door of the hot dog mobile, driving away.

Buck watched him screech off, then he got down on his hands and knees and said, "Dixie Riggs, I would do anything if you'd just come on back home. I'll marry you today if that's what you want. We'll live in our own apartment and everything."

And being the Dixie Riggs that I am, I said, "Well Buck, that's a tempting offer, but I think I'll wait on this marriage thing. After all," I said, turning around to go back into the trailer, lying through my teeth, "I've gotten all kinds of other offers since you've taken your pretty little time."

Buck said, "But Dixie, I thought you wanted to marry me."

I lied, "But Buck, that was before modeling school. Before I saw all the possibilities that lay ahead. You see, my plan is to become a top model. And frankly, I don't see any room in my future for you now. From now on, I'm going to be real busy being a star."

"But Dixie," Buck said, grabbing my arm. He pulled me to him. "I mean it. I'll get Preacher Whatley to marry us today. Right now! Get me the phone. I'll call him this instant."

Glory, the way his eyes were shining like he was about to cry, the way he looked messed up for the first time since I'd known him. The way he was pressing up against me instead of me against him, well, it was all getting to me. I was beginning to feel guilty for being cruel. I was about to die with my great love for him. I was just inches from saying yes yes yes, but then Sparkle came out rubbing her eyes and said, "Dixie, you got any coffee in here? Lord, I've got a hangover. What in the world did I have to drink last night?" Then she opened her eyes wider and took one look at Buck and said, "Oh. It's you. Get lost, why don't you."

For the first time in my natural born life, I was really cruel to Buck. I said, "Well, she's right, you know. How about it. Get lost." And I turned and walked away.

Sparkle was looking under Donnie's couch when I came back in. "What in the hell are you doing?" I asked.

"Looking for some coffee. Take a look at this shit," she said.

I said, "What is it?" I was still shaking, thinking about Buck.

She began pulling all these videotapes out from under the couch, reading the titles: "*Ass Master. Three Hundred and One Big Boobs. Hot Girls and Long— What!* Dixie, this is a real collection he's got going here."

"Are you serious?" I said. "Let me see that."

"No. Wait. Just wait. Listen to this one. This is too good to be true: '*Hot Girls and Long Guys*, the sequel—it's better than the original.' Dixie, you think he's got the original tucked back in there somewhere?" She threw the sequel next to her and started digging towards the back.

There must have been over thirty videos, easy, with a variety of themes. Daddy Speed's collection of magazines paled next to this. Behind the tapes were some of the worst magazines I'd ever seen in my life, dog-eared issues. Sparkle and I laid them all out on the floor by the couch and began looking through every single one of them.

"This is gross, Sparkle. I didn't really go to bed with this guy, did I?"

" 'Fraid so, honey. And get this. This morning when I went into the bathroom to look for toothpaste, I found his medicine chest packed with rubbers."

I groaned. "I thought something funky was going on. Last night I was cleaning up his clothes and there was at least one in every pocket. Different kinds, too. There were so many it was like who are these for? They aren't all for me, are they? I mean, does he make a dry run to the grocery store and say, 'Oh, I'd better take along a condom. Don't know who I might meet?' "

We started laughing, but I wanted a long hot shower. The hickey Donnie had given me the night before felt like it was burning a hole through the back of my neck.

"I can't believe you never saw this stuff," she said. "Don't you bother to snoop?"

"Usually I do. I sure combed Buck's place."

"Yeah, well. Buck wouldn't have anything juicy to find anyway. He's such a bore."

"Shut up, Sparkle. Don't talk about Buck like that."

"Sorry," she said. "Hey, have you ever seen a porno flick before?"

"Never."

"Never? Well, my daddy had loads of them. You got to see at least one."

The tape went in without a hitch. It was already in the middle of the film. We were kneeling in front of it, enthralled, watching all kinds of amazing things. I mean, I'd just had no idea! I'd always thought messing around on Buck was bad. But messing around on Buck was nothing next to this stuff.

"Oh my God, Dixie. I just had the worst thought," said Sparkle. She put her hands up to her face. "Why was this in the middle? What happened? I mean, what happened to him that he had to leave this movie at this point?"

"Oh grossss, Sparkle," I said, groaning, laughing, holding my stomach.

"I knowwwww!" she said. "I bet this is what Roy's like."

"Who's Roy?" I asked.

"You know. The one in the air force?"

"Oh. Yeah." And then I remembered why I was in this mess in the first place, because of those pictures for Roy. "Sparkle. You don't think Trina would send Donnie those pictures, do you?"

"No. I don't even think she knows him," she said. "Oh shit. We'd better look just in case."

We combed the entire trailer looking for any shots of the porno pictures, but we couldn't find any. "Thank goodness for that," she said.

And I said, "No kidding. Could you imagine? This has been the worst week." I hung my head over the side of the bed. Donnie's old construction shoes were there, next to an old bowl of cereal, a pizza box and his six bottles of love potions. "Oh yukkkk," I said.

"What is it?" Sparkle asked, sticking her head under the other side of the bed.

"His sexual cream stash. Hot Oil Rub, Raspberry Love Potion. Oh look, yuk. This bottle's almost empty."

"Grossss!" we said together, cracking up.

"I wonder what he does with this stuff?" said Sparkle.

"I don't even want to know. He didn't use it on me. That's for sure."

"Dixie?"

"What Spark?" I was swinging the ends of my hair back and forth across his floor like a broom. The blood felt good rushing to my face.

"Let's get out of here."

"Sparkle?"

"Yeah, Dix?"

"I'm with you, girl."

I think I'm a redneck. I'm not really sure yet. But I have this sneaking suspicion, standing here in my fake rabbit fur waist-length coat and my black miniskirt, that I am a true redneck. My momma, I am sure, is a redneck. You can see it in the way she walks, the clothes she buys, the different wigs she wears and the way she hits town in the middle of the afternoon, right in the middle of my already screwed-up life. In a word, she is TROUBLE.

She goes to Buck's looking for me. I am not there. She goes to Sparkle's momma's beauty shop looking for me. I am not there. But there she finds her true kindred spirit, Sparkle's momma, Trina. They are two redneck peas in one redneck pod. I am not sure who has more divorces behind them, Trina or Momma, but they hit it off right away, and right away Trina is showing Momma a new way to wear her hair and telling her all about me and Sparkle and our X-rated porno pictures. Momma, I can tell, is pleased with this news. I can just hear the conversation now:

Trina says, "So you're Dixie's mother. Well I'll be. I didn't even know she had one."

And Momma says, "Dixie never has been one to brag about me."

So Trina says, "I've got one just like that in my Sparkle.

And by the way, speaking of those two girls, guess what they've been up to?"

And Momma says, "Do tell?" And by now, Momma is in Trina's chair and Trina is turning Momma this way and that so Momma can look at herself in the mirror from all sides and decide if her hair is tall enough to embarrass me or not.

Trina will go on to explain the whole porno thing, leaving out the fact that it was her idea in the first place, and my momma will be so shocked she will actually forget about herself for one teeninsy little second. She will say, "No! My Dixie? No, huh-uh. Not my girl. Dixie would never have that much fun."

Trina would take her comb and start jabbing it in the top of Momma's hair, saying, "Yes indeedy. Your girl. Naked."

And a big smile would slowly spread across Momma's face and she'd say, "Well I'll be. And to think she used to be such an old stick-in-the-mud." Then she would laugh out loud and before the hairdo would be finished, my momma, LeDaire Riggs Rideout, and her newfound friend, Trina somebody somebody Starling, would already have planned to spend the evening together at one of the local bars featuring Ladies Night Out. They'd take off their latest wedding rings, hike their skirts up a little higher, put on extra concealer, and try to pass for thirty-five.

The reason I knew all this was because Momma was standing right in front of me, all dressed up, laughing. And she was saying, "And then Trina told me about you and Sparkle, and baby," she said, as she hugged me and I pulled away, "baby, it's about fucking time, is all I've got to say."

"Momma," I said, "what are you doing in Myrtle Beach? What happened to Lou?"

And Momma said, "Who?"

"Lou, Momma, Lou? Remember him?"

And she said, "Who?" still laughing like a maniac.

"Oh Momma, come on. You didn't mess that up too?"

"Oh Lord. You've got to loosen up, kid. Don't be so serious. Now listen here, why don't you go on and get yourself dressed up pretty and come with me and Trina tonight."

I had thought I was dressed up pretty. I was standing in front of Renee's World of Fashion Modeling school where Momma had pulled me out of class. No, where she had interrupted class and I had pulled her out onto the doorstep because I didn't want to be seen with her. I was already embarrassed before she came in, because Renee had asked me why I was wearing the same clothes she had previously told me not to wear. Somehow it seemed better saying nothing at all than telling her in front of the whole class that I'd been kicked out of my boyfriend's house and my clothes were all buried somewhere in my car outside my second boyfriend's trailer. And then Momma shows up. I cringed remembering the look on Renee's face. I cringed thinking of the possible look on Buck's face. Oh no, what if Buck had seen my momma? I said, "Momma, who did you talk to at Buck's house?"

And she said, "His mother. And she's the sweetest little woman, Dixie. She invited me in and I had myself a nice cup of hot coffee."

"Momma. You don't drink coffee."

"Of course I don't. But she didn't have anything else. What was I supposed to do?"

"Momma, you didn't go asking her for a drink, did you?"

And Momma said, "Of course I did. I had a roaring headache."

And then I groaned, "Oh Momma, they're good Christian people. Did anyone else see you?"

She threw back her head and laughed again. "No, Dixie. She was the only one."

So then I said, more formally, "I can't come with you tonight, LeDaire. I've got to stay with Sparkle."

"Well bring her along then. There's men enough out there for all of us."

And so I said, "Trina isn't talking to Sparkle. They had a fight over a man."

Momma got that greedy gossipy look in her eyes and whispered, "What happened?"

"Sparkle tried to steal Trina's boyfriend away."

Momma crossed her arms over her tight black knit, practically see-through blouse and said, "Oh. She didn't say anything about that to me. Oh. Well. I see."

"I've got to go on back to class, Momma. Call me tomorrow. And Momma?"

"What baby?"

"Don't you think you ought to change those pants before you go out? They're way too tight."

And Momma did one of those little modeling turns we had just been learning as if it were second nature to her and said, "Honey, I look real good in these pants. I'm not about to change."

"But LeDaire, they're way too tight. You look like a hooker."

She laughed and said, "Honey, you're not on your period again, are you?" and blew me a kiss as she went to get in her car. I didn't even wave good-bye. I went back inside and shut the door as fast as I could. But still I could hear Momma's car squealing out across the gravel. She was laughing up a storm and playing the radio until I just knew that somewhere down the line I must have been switched at birth.

I can tell when I get back to class that everyone's been talking about me behind my back. But I don't care. All I can think about is Buck. All through the runway walks and our three-quarter French military turns, I end up thinking about him. I love him. He loves me. He wants to get married. What had I been thinking of when I'd said no? What had I been thinking of when I'd told him to get lost? I asked myself this as I put one foot in front of the other and did the whole runway routine just the way Renee had done.

She clapped her hands and said, "Darling. Dear. No. Stop. What are you thinking about? Listen to the music. Let it guide you." It was rap music and it was playing loud. The speakers were pounding and buzzing and from what I could hear, some man was rapping about losing his woman.

"Think of your hands, dear," said Renee, clapping hers. "Your hands."

I tried to think of my hands. I tried doing everything Renee had been teaching me. I relaxed my fingertips and displayed my jacket, making sure to show the buttons and the pockets. I tucked my bottom in, sucked in my tummy, kept my shoulders back. But all I could think about was Buck. Me and Buck, we were in love. But when I was ready to marry, he wasn't. When he was ready, I wasn't. And then my momma comes into the picture just in time to really screw things up. She was right on schedule. I knew that once Buck's momma told him what LeDaire was like, Buck would probably think I was lying about those porno pictures being my first and only time. He'd probably think I did that kind of thing for a living. He'd probably think I'd done that kind of thing as a child. He'd probably hear his momma say, "And that horrible woman came prancing in here like a tramp, wearing barely nothing on, wanting a drink. You got to drop that Dixie. She's got bad blood in her. Bad, bad blood."

"Dear, if you can't keep your mind on your work, get off the runway," Renee said, snapping her fingers angrily at me. "Come on, come on. Either do it right or get down."

"No," I said. "I'll do it this time."

I listened to the music. I thought about my hands. I focused on all the photo clippings on the walls of all the models who had been there before me. There were hundreds of shots: small ones, large ones, ones in color, ones in black and white, all glamorous, smiling down on me reminding me of what I was. I was a model. Just like Vanna White, who was everywhere, I was a model. Just like the cover girls up there, I was a model. And just like all the other famous models, I was going to be famous too. Pretty soon I'd be seen in resort commercials, car dealership ads, Pepsi-Cola spots, and before you knew it, I'd even have some magazine covers behind me. I'd be on *Seventeen, Vogue, Glamour.* I'd tape my tits real tight and give them a cleavage and get on the cover of *Cosmopolitan* magazine. I could do it all. There wasn't a question in my mind that I had what it took.

I loosened up my shoulders and held them back and thought about my hands and began my walk down the long, pink runway. This time I gave my routine more spin. I imagined Buck watching me, wanting me, but not being able to have me anymore because I was famous. I went for the extra moves, the light swaying swing of the hips. With one foot in front of the other, I began smiling dirty, naughty, exciting smiles. Then I dipped my shoulders and gave Renee a little "Soul Train," a little Vanna White, a little MTV. I gave her all I had. I didn't know what it was, but I put it in drive and let it kick in. No one was there but me and the runway, and Buck was in my head, wanting me bad, pleading for me to come back, begging for me to come back, as I turned into an Egyptian, angling my hands to the right, then the left, keeping them even with my chin. Then I switched to my hardest move, the full French military turn, the one no one had gotten right all evening. But this time I got it right. And I did it while I grazed my hand down the front of my fake rabbit fur jacket pretending to show off the fur. Finally I surprised even myself by spiraling into a double French military turn. I turned clockwise, then counterclockwise, then I was finished. I looked down at the class. There was no question that I'd done a good job. It was in their eyes. It was in Renee's eyes, too, as she said, "Ummm. Not bad. Not bad." She took a few beats and then a few beats more, not taking her eyes off me, and then she said, "Okay girls. I need you to gather around. I've got something to talk to you about."

That was it? I couldn't believe it. That was all she was going to give me? Not even a "Nice going," or a "Nice turn," or a "Cute hon, but get out of my class." Nothing?

Sparkle patted me on the back when I sat down and said, "Boy, where'd you learn all that from?"

I said, "Shut up."

"Did you get that from your mother? Was that your mother in here? God, she's gorgeous."

"Shut up, Sparkle. I told you to shut up. I don't want to talk about it."

Renee said, "You two, listen up. Now what I need to say might upset some of you and I'm sorry for that. But some things have just got to be said." She walked up onstage and began pacing back and forth. She had a way of talking like she was talking to a basketful of small kittens. And you could tell she loved to hear herself talk. I'd never noticed it before, but I noticed it now, as she prattled on and on and on. She talked about what modeling stood for and how it was a respectable profession and how we shouldn't ever treat it otherwise. She said a woman could do a lot worse than being known for her beauty. She said that most models, like herself, were still considered catches even when they were past their forties. She said that she didn't know of any model, including herself, that couldn't hook herself up with a good millionaire even at the age of fifty or sixty. She said this and then that and then finally she began to wind down and come to the point. "It has come to my attention," she said, "that one of our girls has gotten herself into a little trouble."

I was barely listening. I was wondering where her millionaire was and studying the photo clippings, trying to decide who I looked most like. I was determined not to listen to her. If she couldn't see what I was worth, she didn't have a thing I wanted to hear. Maybe I looked like Vanna White. Only Vanna White had feathered blond hair and mine was straight coal black hair that went down to my thighs. Renee had told me that I'd have to get it cut if I wanted to join her agency.

She went on. "You girls. You get it in your heads that you're going to be some hotshot model and then you go and blow it. Now I understand how you can get such notions. You get a photographer telling you you're the prettiest thing he's ever seen and he's going to make you a star and the next thing you know your clothes are off and your career is over. Ruined."

Suddenly her voice had turned to cold, hard stone and she had my attention all right. I still didn't look at her, because I didn't want her to see my eyes, but she had my full 100 percent attention. Sparkle jabbed me with her elbow, but I kept staring at the walls.

"Here's the deal," Renee said. "If you go nude, you're out. If I find any of you entering any contests without my permission, you're out. If I find any one of you girls at that Tiger Alley Saloon getting yourself wet down or anything, you're out. Understand? Does everyone understand?"

Everyone nodded and Sparkle piped out like a fool, "Yes."

Renee said, "Dixie? You listening?"

"Oh yeah. Sure. I understand."

"Good, because I just won't have it. I just refuse to have that kind of activity in my school." Suddenly her voice changed back to her pouting kitten delivery and she said, "Now I know yall want to have fun. And I can understand why some of you might want to do that kind of thing. But some people don't take it the right way and if it gets around, you can get an awfully bad reputation. Now we don't want that to happen to us, do we?"

We all kind of laughed and nodded, and Renee glided off the runway. Sparkle punched me again. I punched her back. Everyone was quiet, waiting for Renee's next move. She walked right up to me and said, "Dixie, I'd like to see you in my office, please. Now."

Oh Lord. My life in Myrtle Beach had started like a house on fire. Every room was blazing. Then Buck's daddy kicks me out, Donnie takes me in, LeDaire shows up, and now, as I walked the long porno walk back to Renee's office with everyone watching me walking, I felt like I was holding a match with my hand over it to keep it from blowing out.

"Yeah. Okay," I said, dying as Renee closed the door. "What's up?" My voice was shaking. I was shaking.

"Dixie?"

"Yes ma'am?"

She sat down at her desk and started thumbing through her files. I waited for her to pull out the photos. I'd just deny them. Or I'd use that superimposing line. Or I'd get mad at her. Or I'd cry. Or maybe I'd laugh and say, "Well what do you know? I've got tits."

She said, "Dixie, this is very hard for me to do." She didn't even look at me. She just handed me the folder. I was shaking harder now, reaching for it. I wasn't about to open it. I figured I'd wait and see what she had to say first. One thing was for sure, I didn't have to look at the pictures to hear what she had to say.

"Dixie," she said. She picked up a paper clip and began bending it out of shape. I stood there waiting, hoping she'd chip her perfect pink nail polish. "I'm afraid, Dixie, that you're going to have to think about coming back next semester, when you have more money."

"Next semester? What are you talking about? I can't wait to do that. I've got to be a model now." I opened the folder, expecting the photos. I hadn't expected a crummy bill for $265. Then I remembered the registration fee, the makeup fee. I wasn't a porno queen after all. I was just broke. "Oh Renee, I'm really sorry. I just forgot to bring it, is all. I'll bring it next time." I was so happy, I didn't know what I was saying.

"Are you sure?" Her voice became sweet again.

"Yes, I'm sure," I said. "Gosh, I'm so sorry."

"It's okay. I just can't let these things slip, you know. Usually Casey does this kind of work, but with her gone, well, I just hate dealing with money matters like this."

"Casey's gone?" I asked, shocked.

Suddenly she reached out and grabbed me. She threw her arms around me like Momma was always trying to do, only I didn't pull away from Renee.

She said, "Oh honey. I know how upset it makes you. But don't you worry about Casey. She knew the rules. I can't have people thinking yall come out of here posing nude for every Tom, Dick or Harry. This is not a Playboy Club. Somebody has to protect you girls. Now listen here. You bring your money next class, because I don't want to end up losing you. You've got something really different. Really special. You know, I see a lot of Vanna White when I look at you."

"Vanna White!" I said. This was the best possible news. Wait until Buck heard about this.

"Yes. You don't have the same coloring, but you have the same facial expressions. I was her teacher, you know."

"I know. Everyone knows that. You're the best."

Then she turned me around and looked at me hard and said, "Come to think of it, I might just take you up to New York with me next time I go. I'm taking five of my best girls at the end of the program. How tall are you, anyway?"

"Five feet, eight inches tall."

She said, "No. More like five seven. That's not great, but it's okay. Do you know what size shoe you wear?"

"I don't know. Somewhere around a seven." My feet were the worst part of my body. They were so small. I always bought bigger shoes to hide them because they looked so deformed to me.

Renee said, "Take your shoes off, please."

I did not want to do this. But I sat down anyway and took them off. Renee picked each one of my feet up separately.

She studied them. She put them together, lining up the right toes with the left toes, the left heel with the right one. And then she got a measuring tape out of her desk and measured everything: toe to heel, side to side, sole to arch, and she did it to each foot, writing down all the measurements.

"Renee," I said, cracking up. "Please stop. You're tickling me!"

"Hold still." She was very serious. Finally she dropped the tape measure on the floor. She flipped through her notes. She made more notes and compared those. Then she looked up at me and said, "Dixie, are you aware that you have a perfect size-six foot?"

Suddenly I got mad. "No, I don't," I said. "I wear a size seven." I don't know why I got mad. I just did. I was burning up inside. It was like in saying that, she was trying to hide what was really wrong with me. It was the same thing as telling a man that his blind date has beautiful eyes when she's really a fatty. What she was trying to tell me was that I had nice feet but I'd never make it as a model.

"Honey," she said, "I'd pay a lot of money to have feet like yours. You're a natural. I don't want to lose you. So you take care of that bill. And listen here, do you think you could get rid of that coat?"

"Sure." I laughed. I cooled down fast, embarrassed that I'd gotten so upset. Renee was going to make me a star, and if she liked my feet, she could have them.

We walked out of her office laughing, into the pink modeling room with the pink runway and all the mirrors and photographs. The rap music had turned into a slow Madonna number and all the girls were looking at me, expecting me to head for the door. Instead I held my head high and smiled at them all. They looked disappointed, but I didn't care. I focused on the clippings on the wall. They'd better start making plans to move on over and make room for me because I had plans to take over their spots. And then, like a bad joke put on this earth just to bring me down to size, I saw the one thing I could not take. The one thing that made me weaker than anything. The one thing that seemed to taunt me wherever I went. It was over in the upper left-hand corner of the wall. It was a very small version of the very same picture of Paulette. The very same picture I'd stolen from above Buck's bed.

Sparkle said, "You okay, Dixie? What's wrong? What'd she say? Did she find the photographs?"

"Look, everything's fine. Everything's going to be okay."

But it wasn't. LeDaire was in town. Buck was gone. Paulette was on the wall. And my feet were just too damned small. And then it hit me. My stupid friend Sparkle, with her flat face, no features to speak of and no ambitions of ever being a model, had four inches' height on me and a better shot at making it as a model than I ever did. Lord, nothing's fair in this world.

19

When me and Sparkle left modeling class that evening, the first thing we saw was my sweet Buck waiting outside the front door. I couldn't believe it. First my momma and then Buck and before you knew it my Methodist grandmother would probably show up from the grave looking almost as glum as Buck was, standing there scratching things in the sand with his perfect canvas loafers.

Sparkle said, "What the hell are you doing here, creep? Get lost," because she couldn't stand him.

And he said, ignoring her, "Dixie, come on girl, we got to talk."

And me, with my heart pounding, said, "No. We don't got to do anything except go home and change. I've got a big date tonight."

Buck looked at me hard, like he was studying me, only somewhere in that stare was the hollow empty look of a man done wrong. I felt like running up to him, flinging my arms around him and saying, "Baby, baby, baby, you know I love only you. Just forget what I said and take me back and make me your wife." But I knew Buck. He'd say okay and be super nice for two days and then forget I'd ever been gone. He'd never marry me then. How does that old saying go? Something like, why buy the cow if you get the milk for free?

Something like that. So instead I just said, "Well, see you around kiddo."

Buck said, "Dixie?"

And I said, cheerfully "Gotta go now, bye-bye." I sounded just like my mother, making even me sick. I slid into Sparkle's car the model way, the way Renee had taught us, where you sit down on the car seat sideways, then lift your feet keeping your ankles together and kind of swivel around like a lazy Susan until you come to rest facing the dashboard. Who came up with these ideas?

My heart was going Ba-Boom Ba-Boom Ba-Boom, and the blood in my veins was rushing around my head sounding like a speedboat. It's times like these, when you'll do just about anything to calm down, that someone like Sparkle can really come along and mess things up. Things were already messed up, but now they were going to be even more messed up. I knew the minute she got in her side of the car and started pulling out of the parking lot saying, "Dixie, have you ever thought about entering any contests before," that I was about to get into some big, big trouble.

So I said, "Wait a minute. Remember what Renee said."

So Sparkle said, "Renee shma-nay. How the hell would she ever find out? Do you think she ever even leaves that modeling palace of hers? And besides, she's the one who put the idea into my head in the first place. I wouldn't have even thought of it if it hadn't been for her. So what do you say, Dixie?"

I was thinking, "I wonder if Buck's following me. Maybe he is. Maybe he's right behind me and is going to keep on my tail until he gets me back." All my energy was right there hoping that, so I just didn't have the strength to go a couple of rounds with Sparkle on what was wrong and what was right. She's so stubborn. Once she's got it in her head to do something, she'll get in a fight with you if you say no.

So I said, "Okay Sparkle, but what kind of contest are you talking about, exactly?"

She said, "You know. A contest, contest."

No, I did not know. But something told me I was going to

find out, as Sparkle gunned her T-Bird off the Ocean Boulevard heading towards the King's Highway.

"One thing's for sure," she said, adjusting her rearview mirror. "If Buck Speed thinks he can follow us around all night, he's got another think coming."

"Sparkle!" I turned around just in time to see him not make the turn in time with us. "Sparkle, that wasn't nice. Come on. Go back and get him."

"Dixie, you got to learn to drop that boy. If he's so all-fire great, why didn't you marry him? Huh? Answer me that?"

It was hard enough facing up to the fact that Buck didn't want to marry me, without having to tell Sparkle about it. So I had kind of lied. I had kind of said to her, "Sparkle, I can't see spending the rest of my life with him. He's just not what I had in mind. He's nice and all, but." Then I had added, "And I just had to leave. If he had asked me to marry him one more time, I would have crawled out of my skin."

☆

Buck aside, some men are just real creeps. And one way to find out is to spend two hours at a Laundromat heating you up a pair of jeans in a hot dryer, squeezing them on trying not to let the zipper burn you, and walking over to the Tiger Alley Saloon and out onto a stage in a pair of four-inch high heels with a paper bag over your head so the judges can't see your face. It is like: "Hoot hoot," "Oooh, Momma Momma," "Honey don't you want to come and spend the night with me!"

First prize was a trip to Hawaii for two. Second prize was that three hundred dollars I was going to need to pay Renee off for modeling school and makeup.

Sparkle whispered, "Dixie, remember, when it's your turn to walk the runway, tone it down. You don't want to come in first."

Sparkle tells me all the time that I have an ass men would die for. She does not mind this because she has legs that just keep going, going, going, up and up and up. She could win a short shorts contest in a minute.

The emcee, Charlie Enlow from WAVE radio station 102.7,

was hosting the competition. We were on a runway, not unlike the runway at Renee's, only it wasn't pink, it was black, and there weren't any mirrors, there were just wall-to-wall men. They hugged the stage as Charlie called each one of us out using our fake names and fake occupations. Trixie worked as a rocket scientist by day, by night she modeled. Roxanne was a neurosurgeon. Alicia excavated anthropological digs and didn't everyone dig her? Yes, uh-huh! It was that sort of thing.

"Number Twenty-seven," Charlie Enlow called out. It was Sparkle's number. She was up. "Number Twenty-seven is a tall, good looking pilot who flies jets for a commercial airlines," Charlie said, pretending he was flying the jet. Sparkle walked past him and went down the stage like a plane about to land. Then she did one of Renee's turns badly, and walked back swinging her hips. She had a good shot at the Hawaiian trip.

Then it was my turn, Number 28. I was Luanne from Lithuania, new to the state and practicing international law. I tried to tuck my hair in my pants so no one would recognize me. It was much longer than the paper bag. I pressed in my stomach, tucked in my rear end, pulled my shoulders back and tried desperately to keep from swinging my hips. But it's like all my friends tell me, "Dixie Riggs, if you took a perfectly round serving bowl and sat in it, you would fill it up completely and beautifully. No one has such a gorgeous ass." I knew there was no way I could lose. I knew I was going to win that first-place trip, when what I needed was that second-place money so desperately. I should have taken the money Buck had tried to offer. I should have asked my momma for money. But there wasn't any way I would have done that. But I should have taken the money from Buck. I walked slow, real slow, trying to keep everything still.

Charlie Enlow said, "Good golly, Miss Molly. You can make it. Come on."

The audience laughed. I walked even slower. I wanted to run, but I wanted that second place more.

Charlie said to the audience, "These slow Lithuanian types are known for their brains. They come from a land that is blah, blah, blah," was all that I could hear as I got to the foot of the runway and looked out over the crowd through the slits in my paper bag. Every man in the place was laughing, talking, drinking beer, pointing. They were everywhere, with their big old faces and hairy hands and T-shirts and cigarettes, and one guy even had a tattoo of a mermaid covering his entire arm. I could feel my hair swinging out of my jeans. I began breathing hard. And then I saw Buck. He was sitting a little to the right, next to the side bar, glaring at the stage. "Good God!" I thought. "He'll kill me if he sees me up here." I immediately turned around and started back, but not before some creep reached up and grabbed my ass.

I shouted, "Get your hands off me you slimy son of a bitch."

He hollered, "Hey baby, come on down here," and he reached up and grabbed my hair.

"Go to hell you jerk," is what I told him.

Buck was on him in an instant, pushing him away, saying, "Dixie, get off that stage now!"

I said, "Leave me alone," to both of them. The bouncer, a bodybuilding type bigger even than Buck, came up and grabbed them both.

Charlie Enlow laughed and said, "Okay gentlemen, that was our last contestant. Judges, add up your scores and turn in your cards. We're going to have a hot winner tonight."

The last I saw of Buck was the bouncer escorting him away from the bar. I was crushed. There he was one minute, trying to protect me, and the next, he was being kicked out. I felt horrible. I knew he'd leave me now for good. Who wouldn't? He'd been pushed too far. But maybe I could get him back. I'd get that trip to Hawaii and take him with me. Yeah. That's what I'd do. Him and me and all those beautiful Hawaiian beauties serving us piña coladas. We'd windsurf and sail in the moonlight and Buck would say, "Dixie, why don't we just get married right here. Right now." And it would just so happen that we'd be on one of those dinner boats where you go out around seven, eat, cruise the blue Pacific and come back at ten. And we'd have the captain marry us right there on the dance floor, with everyone eating their desserts. We'd be Mr. and Mrs. Buck Speed by the time we got back to shore. I'd forget modeling and settle down to have Buck Speed, the Fourth. I'd even try and get along with my momma. I had to think this way. It was the only way to think as I thought of Buck, climbing back in that truck he was painting, going home to his family to tell them that, yes, I really did take after my mother, and wasn't it a good thing he had found out before it was too late?

Sparkle said, "Did you see Buck?"

"Sparkle, can't you ever shut up?"

Charlie Enlow said, "Okay, the fourth runner-up wins a free dinner for two at Slug's Rib House. Number Nineteen, step on up here."

Number 19 walked up to Charlie. The audience hooted and dog-whistled. Charlie took the paper bag off her head and gave her a kiss on the cheek. There was even more whistling. Then Charlie Enlow gave Number 19 two tickets and she beamed at him. Charlie pointed to his side and whispered, "Step on over this way, honey." Then he called out, "Okay, our third runner-up wins a Sony CD Walkman. Let's see. Our third runner up is . . ." He opened an envelope and said, "Ah-ha! Number Twenty-eight, come on up here. Where are you, you Lithuanian goddess, you?"

I was Number 28. That was me, Number 28. Number 28 was me, third place. A Walkman. Surely this was a joke. Charlie patted me on the ass and took off my bag and the audience went crazy, stomping their feet like they were at a football game.

The rest was a blur. Sparkle didn't even win a handshake. And the girls that won first and second place were true barking dogs. Even Donnie Sessions wouldn't go out with women like that. Even Donnie, for all his sleazy ways, had a limit to ugliness.

Two of the judges, hailing from New Jersey, came right up to me and Sparkle the minute we walked off the stage. They introduced themselves. "My name's Richard," said the tallest one with the big college ring on his finger, "and this guy with all the gold around his neck is Jerry. You two look like you need a drink."

I said, "Hey you jerks. How come yall picked those creepy girls over us? What are you, blind?" I slammed my Walkman down on the table and began to walk away.

The man with the ring grabbed me. "Whoa, whoa there. Hold on now. We didn't want you going anywhere, that's all. We've got bigger plans for you."

"Oh right," I said.

"Calm down. Why don't you gals come have a drink on us and listen to what we've got to say?"

The guy with the gold necklaces said, "Yeah. We don't know many people around here."

"Oh puh-lease!" I said. "That's the worst line I've ever heard. Got anything else original?"

"Yeah. Hey, you going through your midlife crisis, or what?" asked Sparkle. She reached up and flipped his gold chains. "You know, these things went out about ten years ago, buddy. Dixie, maybe he's got some nice parachute pants at home."

"Yeah, maybe I do." He smiled. "Maybe you'd like to come home and watch me put them on."

"Gross," said Sparkle.

The man with the college ring cracked up and said, "That's what I like. A couple Southern girls with spunk. Look here, we've been working for hours and we could really use a drink." He began pulling stuff out of his pocket. Right away I noticed that he had a shiny gold money clip just about to explode with hundred-dollar bills, enough money to keep me in modeling school for a century. "Here," he said, giving me his business card. "Once again. I'm Richard. This here is Jerry. We're in boats and we've got a business proposition to talk over with you. So what you say? Is there a better place to go around here for a drink?"

"Well, maybe," I said, "but first I got to go get something at this shop."

"Okay, just lead the way." He adjusted his white tie and patted his friend on the shoulder.

I didn't bother to introduce us. I just walked out the bar and kept on going. Sparkle rolled her eyes at me and I hooked my head for her to come on. "Let's have some fun," I whispered to her, as they followed behind. "Let's get even with those bastards. Imagine picking those dogs over us."

"No kidding," said Sparkle. "How do you think I felt? I didn't even fucking place."

We went through the back entrance of the Gay Dolphin Souvenir Shop and Sparkle pointed at the door. "Stand there. Don't move," she said to them. "What fucking goons!" she said to me, rolling her eyes again.

I said, "Did you get a load of their pants? That one guy's pants don't even reach his ankles and the other one, I don't know what's wrong with his, but it's something horrible."

"Sans-a-Belt," said Sparkle, "a golfer's dream. My granddaddy used to wear them."

We went over to the Myrtle Beach T-shirts and began picking them up and spreading them out across our chests. MY WIFE RAN OFF WITH MY BEST FRIEND AND I MISS HIM. HONK IF YOU LOVE JESUS. HONK IF YOU THINK I'M CUTE. WHAT YOU SEE MAY BE WHAT

YOU WANT BUT YOU SURE AIN'T GOING TO GET IT. We held them up and smiled at Richard and Jerry and they smiled back.

"Gross," I said, "they love this crap."

"Yeah," said Sparkle, "I sure hope you don't think I'm going out with those yayhoos. They look like a couple a Jaycees."

"But did you see those hundred-dollar bills that Richard guy's toting around?" I said. "I could get me a penthouse based on his money clip alone."

"I didn't see any money," said Sparkle. "Are you lying again?"

"I never lie," I said.

"Yeah. Right."

"Okay, watch this." I couldn't resist. I picked up a large owl that was made of glued-on seashells. I held it out to them and said in my tackiest Southern accent, "Don't yall just love this. I want one of these so bad."

"Oh yuk!" Sparkle said, kind of squealing under her breath. "You're horrible."

"I know. But somehow if they buy this, I'll like them better." I yelled again. "Don't yall just love it? I really love it. I'd kill for one of these things." I was pointing at the owl like a maniac.

Jerry and Richard bobbed their heads up and down, and Jerry nudged Richard, who pulled out his money clip again.

"See," I said, "I wasn't lying. Go on, get something girl. Let's get a lot of stuff and make them pay for all of it."

A half hour later we were telling them our names and heading out for the Pavilion, with Jerry and Richard carrying one lava lamp, my owl, a Mickey Mouse beach towel, one shark's-tooth necklace, two string bikinis, and two I LOVE MYRTLE BEACH T-shirts that we made them buy for themselves and put on. They really did look like goons.

We rode every ride at least once and then rode them one more time. The plan was to let Richard and Jerry have a really good time with us, promising them a night of hot passion, and then go to the ladies' room and sneak out the back; maybe even leaving them a false address, thereby causing them as much trouble as they caused me by cheating me out of my three-hundred-dollar prize. I still couldn't believe it. There wasn't going to be any way to get Buck back now. And if they thought we believed that crap about them having a proposal for us, well, we weren't stupid. We knew what that proposal was.

Richard, the tallest one, was somewhat of a gentleman but Jerry wouldn't leave Sparkle alone. He kept putting his arm around her on every roller coaster dip, every dragon chamber turn, every time the Ferris wheel stopped at the top with the seat rocking back and forth. Then it began to get late and we had us a couple a hot dogs.

"So what did you say you did again?" I asked Richard, spreading mustard on my bun. "You're awfully tall."

"We're into boats. We used to be basketball players, but now we're into boats. As a matter of fact, we're in charge of running this big convention in town." He had already started on his second hot dog before I'd even bit into my first.

"Yeah," said Jerry, as he put his arm around Sparkle again.

She wasn't having any of it. "How about you quit, you creep," she said. "I'm only seventeen."

"Right," he said, winking at her.

"See," said Richard, ignoring Jerry. "There's this big boat convention in town. We manage the Speed-O Boat Company and we needed to find us a couple of models. Of course the minute we laid eyes on you girls—"

"I've never heard of Speed-O Boats," I said. "Sparkle, you ever heard of Speed-O Boats?"

"Nope."

"Well, you want to go to the ladies' room with me?"

Sparkle's eyes lit up. "I thought you'd never ask."

"Well hold on," Jerry said, putting his arm around her once more. "Think on this while you're in there. We pay a good price for a day's worth of modeling. No strings attached. That is, unless you want some strings attached." He squeezed her again and gave her a greasy smile.

"You are so disgusting," she said. "I bet you've got a flaming red sports car out front with a license plate that reads

I'M RED HOT." She ducked under his arm, taking his hand with her, and twisted it as hard as she could. "Well, is that hot enough for you Mr. Midlife Crisis? Huh?"

He faked pain. "Oh. Oh."

"Your friend's pretty funny," Richard said, pointing to Sparkle. "But Jerry's right. We pay good money for top modeling."

These words cast Richard and Jerry into a new light for me. Actually, if I stepped back and looked at them from a certain angle, they weren't half bad looking. In fact, they were both pretty good looking. They were real tall, but they were good looking.

"Okay, we'll think about it," I said. "Come on, Spark."

"It's about time," she said, as we went into the bathroom. She pulled out her lipstick and began circling her mouth. "I thought we'd never get rid of those guys."

"Well Sparkle," I said. "What do you think about that modeling stuff? Don't you think it's a good idea?"

"Dixie," she said. She stared at me hard. "Those guys just reek of hard up."

"Well, let's just see what they've got to offer. It can't hurt to see what they've got to offer."

I did not realize what a slut I was until I woke up the next morning. I had slept through my trashiness. There were room-service trays all over the place. It looked like I'd had a dinner party for eight. Without picking my head up too high off the pillow I could count seven bottles of wine—seven!—and one was a bottle of champagne.

I shook Sparkle awake. The red button on the phone was blinking, but the phone was off the hook now. The curtains were open and the morning sun was shining right in my eyes—eyes that had seen a lot of smoke the night before. How many places had we gone last night? Where were they? Who were we with when we went there and how many people were with us? And who in the hell had paid for everything? I saw the lava lamp on the floor and the Mickey Mouse towel draped over the mirror. For a minute I thought whoever we were with had paid for everything. Then I saw a receipt. It was my handwriting all right. But I'd signed it Gladys Speed.

The room service menu had chocolate cake smeared on it and it said we were at the Waikiki–Myrtle Beach Hotel. The operator said the message was from Reno.

"Reno?" I asked.

"Yes," she said. "He told me to tell you that your outfits

could be picked up at the front desk and to be there no later than ten."

"My outfits?" Suddenly I remembered. We were going to do some modeling for Richard.

"What time is it now?" I asked.

"Ten minutes of," the operator said.

"Shit." I hung up the phone. "Sparkle, do you remember where he said we were supposed to go?"

"No." She rubbed her eyes. "I don't even remember what we were supposed to do."

"The boat show. We're going to model at the boat show, remember?"

"Oh. Yeah."

"Well get up then."

The maid knocked on the door and I yelled, "Ten minutes. God, where's all my stuff? What in the hell am I doing? Look at all these trays! Did we really eat all this?"

"All of it," said Sparkle, turning over in bed, groaning.

Sometimes when you can't remember anything, everything will suddenly come slamming back at you. I could close my eyes and see it all clearly now. Me, sitting on top of Richard's lap, rubbing his hair, telling him he wouldn't be half bad if he'd just change his name to Reno, kissing his ring, asking if I could borrow it for a while. And Buck, walking in right at that moment, catching the whole thing. But where had we been? I couldn't remember that part. But I remembered looking up into Buck's great big sexy green eyes and me saying, "Oh hey, baby. Pull up a seat. Me and Reno, here, are going to dance."

And him saying, "Come on, Dixie. I'm taking you home."

And me saying, "Home is where the heart is and my heart's out on that dance floor. Let's go, Reno."

And Sparkle saying, "Well if it isn't Buck Speed the bore. What hole did you crawl out from?"

And Buck sitting there while me and Reno danced and danced and danced until that is all I can remember. The last thing I can see is that reflector ball going around and around making spots of colored light on all my clothes. Oh, yeah. And me saying, "Let's just order up one of everything. That way we don't have to make any decisions." Somewhere in there was a small time lapse I couldn't quite account for.

"Oh Lord, Sparkle," I said, trying to get up. "What happened last night?"

"Don't ask me," she said. "All I know is they said they were big guns at this boat convention and we told them we were famous models and everybody was lying to everybody and then Buck walked in and I told him to get lost and then I was kissing him and you were off throwing up somewhere."

"You were kissing Buck? My Buck?"

"Unfortunately."

"Did you do anything else? Oh no, did I do anything else, like with those guys?"

"Well," said Sparkle, rolling over again, pulling the sheet over her face, "I sure as hell didn't sleep with those two creeps. You might have, but I didn't. Gross, I still can't believe I was kissing Buck."

She groaned and I checked my clothes. My panty hose were still on. That was always a good sign. It wasn't like they were hanging off the corner of the TV.

The phone rang again. "I forgot," the operator said. "There's one more message for you. A Mr. Buck Speed has been trying to ring you all morning. He says it's urgent."

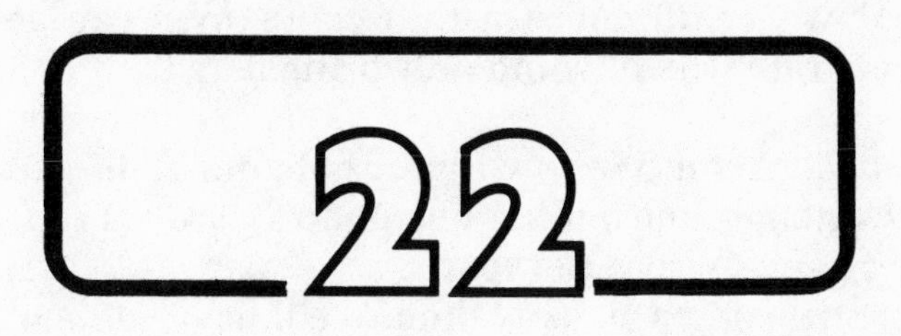

I was not about to call Buck. The total charge to his momma's Visa came to $219 plus tax, not including the charges I'd run up at Newberry's Department Store. That, plus the $265 I owed to modeling school was going to set me back into deep, deep trouble. No. I couldn't quite see calling Buck.

We decided not to check out. Me and Sparkle decided to stay another day and try and come up with the money so they wouldn't run Momma Speed's Visa charge through. Somehow, in my foggy hungover head, it seemed like we could raise that kind of money that fast. I knew top New York models cleared two thousand dollars, hell, even ten thousand dollars a day. So I figured we had a good shot at about five hundred dollars apiece modeling for Reno. We'd pay off our bills and have enough left over to get us an apartment together.

The front desk said okay to staying, but that they'd have to move us to a bigger, more expensive room because the room we were staying in was already reserved for another guest. "Is that okay?" asked the reservation girl. "It's a suite." She had long frosted nails and was wearing the coral blue uniform of a Waikiki–Myrtle Beach employee.

I said, "How much more is it?"

She said, "Let me see." She punched in a few keys on her

computer with a pencil and came back with, "Thirty dollars more. However, if you're with a company, I can get you a corporate rate which would only bring it up to fifteen dollars more."

So I said, "Yeah. We're with . . . hold on." I dug around in my pocketbook and pulled out Reno's card. "Yeah, here it is. The Speed-O Boat Company."

Then she said, "Oh, okay then. We'll have someone move your luggage for you, if that's all right?"

We didn't have any luggage that I knew of. "Hey," I said, "did two men leave some outfits here for us? Two tall men? The operator said they left them here."

Thirty minutes later, forty-five minutes late, me and Sparkle arrived at the boat show convention hall wearing green-and-yellow-striped jackets over yellow-and-green polka-dotted string bikinis. On our heads were two big bright pink hats that had SPEED-O BOATS 1990! printed across the bright green hatbands. But still, the security guard wouldn't let us in the door.

"Why not!" I demanded.

"Because you don't have no pass," he said. He was working his way through a box of saltwater taffy.

"Yeah. Well how about you just telling Richard and Jerry that we're here."

He said, "Who the hell are they?"

"For your information, mister, they run this operation."

"Well, I ain't never heard of them. You got their last names or something?"

He had me there. I dug around in my pocketbook and brought out Reno-Richard's card again. "Yeah, okay. It's Clayton. Richard Clayton."

"Like I said, never heard of them. Let me see that card." He took the card and looked at it for a long, long time. Then he scanned it down against the names on the registration list. "They ain't here, but I can see by their card they're in boats. Well, go on in then. But listen here. You don't tell nobody I let you in. You understand?"

The place was huge. Even by Myrtle Beach standards it was big. And it was glamorous. There were bright lights and streamers everywhere. Everything glistened and everything looked like chrome. And everywhere you turned there were tall, gorgeous women wearing old Southern plantation dresses, or cream knit dresses with bone-colored shoes. These fancy dressed-up women were walking people back and forth, showing off the line of boats they represented.

There were a lot of boats. Whole fleets lined up at the same angle as if they were already in the water, sailing off into the sunset. Then, under yellowish lighting and at a different angle than all the other boats, way, way over in the far, far corner, lined up against the wall like they might belong to drug smugglers, were three motorboats with the driver's seats high in the air. They weren't much larger than that. They were certainly smaller than anything else being featured, but their banner was larger than any other banner around. Larger and louder, in a bright neon pink it read: SPEED-O BOATS—YOUR BOAT TO THE FUTURE. CATCH THE WAVE.

Me and Sparkle looked at each other. We were the only models in the whole place wearing bikinis.

"Yeah, I know," said Reno, when I went up to him and said, "Has it come to your attention yet that no other women in this place is wearing a bathing suit?"

"Yeah, you son of a bitch," Sparkle said. "You better talk real fast, or I've got a couple of redneck boyfriends that are just a phone call away from doing a good job on you."

"Look girls. It was your idea. Remember? We talked it all over last night." He looked at me and raised his eyebrow, smiling. I cringed. It seemed like everything was coming back to me but the stuff that had to do with him. I had completely blacked out there. We could have driven up and down country roads doing it in the back of his car all night long while Jerry watched, and I wouldn't have remembered. Lord, I hoped I wasn't such a slut.

"Don't you remember?" he asked again. "I told you they'd stuck us back in this corner and that we had to figure out a way to get people back here, and you said you two could wear bikinis. Remember?"

My head was singing it hurt so bad. I didn't remember that.

"Well, trust me," he said, looking me straight in the eye.

"The whole thing was your idea. My idea was to have you wear this." He opened a box on the floor and pulled out a cheerleader outfit.

"I'd rather wear that," said Sparkle.

Jerry came running up from out of nowhere. He had twice as many gold chains on as the night before. "Hey hot girl," he said, winking at me. "Some hot night, huh?"

I groaned. Surely I had left Jerry alone the night before.

"Well, maybe we can play a little more after we get some work done, heh? Come on. You girls take off your jackets. Here come some customers." He slapped me on the butt and clapped his hands for us to speed things up, and just as fast as he'd come out of nowhere, he had disappeared back into it.

"You got to be out of your mind, Reno," Sparkle said. "This jacket's staying on."

"Yeah," I said. "I don't care what I told you. You wear the bathing suits. I'm going home."

Reno pulled out his money clip and gave us fifty dollars each. "Come on, gals. There's a lot more where this came from. Just do me this one little favor and we'll work everything out later." He wasn't even paying attention to us. He was begging us while he went over some paperwork.

I said, "Did you know that guy at the front gate hadn't ever even heard of you? Seems to me like if you were running this show, he'd at least have known who you were."

Two men and a woman went up to the boats and ran their hands along the sides and Reno looked up from his paperwork to us and said, "Well, I didn't want to tell you girls this because I didn't want you to get your hopes up, but a friend of mine, a talent scout for a New York modeling agency, is going to be coming into town tonight and if you'll just do me this one favor, I'll see what I can do about setting you up an appointment with him." He looked at the customers and then back at us. "What do you say?"

I didn't know if we were being taken in or what, but me and Sparkle each crawled up on separate boats and took off our jackets and stretched out across the bow like we were suntanning down by the Pavilion. It really wasn't half bad until Jerry got back from whatever hole he had crawled out from under and started hanging around, talking to us, touching us. He had an oiliness about him that kept most of the customers from coming over to whatever boat he happened to be leaning on at the time. But Reno would swoop down on those customers with his stacks of literature and give them his pitch, at the end of which he would tell them he was going in the back to get them a free gift. Then he'd signal for me and Sparkle, and we'd jump down off the bow and walk the clients around the boat one more time in our bikinis. Sparkle would show them the outside and I'd take them up and show them all around the inside. Then Reno would hand us these free presents, things like calculators, watches and alarm clock radios for us to hand to them and then it was back on the bows for us. We sold one boat the whole day.

Finally a bell went off and the convention lights were replaced by the softer lights of closing time. That's when me and Sparkle went up to Reno and said, "Okay, so how much did we make?"

Reno said, "I already gave you fifty dollars. That's more than most girls get doing two of these shows."

I said, "Wait a minute here. Fifty dollars? You've got to be joking."

Reno flattened his lips and shook his head.

So Sparkle said, "But you told us there was more where that came from."

Reno said, "Yeah. But that was providing you girls sold some boats. You only sold one. You work on commission in this business." He turned back to look at his papers again.

Sparkle said, "Well you son of a bitch. You didn't say anything about no commission."

I said, "Reno, come on now. We worked really hard." Then Jerry started walking over, hitching up his pants, and I said, "We should at least get something more for putting up with that jerk."

Reno looked up and laughed. "Okay, okay. I'll give you ten dollars more apiece."

"Ten dollars!" we said together.

"You got to be kidding," I said. "What kind of racket is this anyway?"

"Ten dollars," said Reno. "And like I said, I'm going to get you an appointment with that talent scout. You girls meet me at the Tiger Alley tonight around eleven. And wear something short. This man likes legs."

Jerry heard the word "legs" as he came up and started grinning and looking ours up and down.

Sparkle said, "Quit looking at me you creep. You haven't quit drooling all day."

"You two didn't mind me looking so much last night." He grinned.

"Come on, Reno. Look at him." I groaned. "Twenty dollars, okay? We earned at least twenty dollars."

Reno pulled out his money clip and said, "Fifteen dollars and I'll see you tonight."

There was one message from Donnie Sessions when we got back to the Waikiki, two from my mother, and fifteen messages from Buck Speed.

Sparkle said, "Damn! They must have gotten these bathing suits from the preteens' department. Look at the lines they cut in my skin." She stuck her hip out at me and rubbed it. "We gave them this bikini idea my ass. Hey, you going to call Buck?"

"Hell no," I said. "I don't even know how he knows I'm here."

Sparkle said, "Well, if I were you, I'd go ahead and call him. You never know what he might want."

I said, "I thought you hated him."

"I do. I'm just curious."

So I picked up the phone and dialed his number and immediately got Momma Speed. The minute she heard my voice, she went on and on in a stream of good tidings. "Well hey, sweetie. How are you? We just been missing you so much. Me and Daddy Speed wanted you and your momma to come have dinner with us tonight. I can barely wait to see you. The house hasn't been the same since you left. It's so lonely. Poor old Buck's been trying to reach you all day. He's about to go out of his mind. Did he finally get you?"

All I could think about was her Visa card. How could I

have done that to her? No one was as nice as Momma Speed. I said, "Momma Speed, I would love to have dinner with you. But I don't think my momma can come. She's going out of town."

"No, she's not dear. She said she'd be here at six-thirty on the dot. She's even bringing a date."

"A date. Who?"

"I'm not really sure," Momma Speed said. "I think it's someone she just met recently. But she's so pretty, she probably never has any problem meeting nice men."

This was worse than all my money problems combined. When I hung up I said, "Sparkle, what am I going to do?"

Sparkle said, "He's probably going to be real nice. You want me to come?"

"Glory, no! You and Buck in the same room while I'm worrying about Momma? I'd have me a heart attack."

She said, "I'll be okay. Come on, Dix. You need me now."

"Are you sure? I know how much you hate being around Buck."

And she said, "Dixie. What are friends for?"

I used to always ask Momma, I'd say, "LeDaire, did you really want to get married or did you just have to because of me?" I know she always lied when she told me that it was what she had wanted. I could tell by all the men she did not stay married to.

First there was my daddy. His name was Laymen Riggs. He wasn't much, you can tell that much by his name. He drove an eighteen-wheeler that LeDaire said had a plastic shield over the hood that read: MUFF MAN. Is this, I ask you, the kind of man you'd want your momma marrying? Mostly he transported pine logs from South Carolina to Georgia. But Momma says those miles kept dwindling down until mostly all he did was just sit around and look good. I have seen pictures of this man, Laymen. We have the same eyes, the same sleek black hair and the same crooked smile.

Anyway, LeDaire got tired of his lazy ways and left him for Earl-Dad. Well, that's what I used to call him anyway. Earl-Dad was a locksmith. His office was in a blue van, where he did master keying, rekeying, residential keying, any kind of keying you wanted. On any given day you could walk by a house or a hotel and see him in the parking lot through his dusty rearview window working on those machines. The thing I remember most about Earl-Dad was that he had this black Scottish terrier named Boy, who was always running away. Every time I saw that dog it was two or three hundred feet down the road from our house. One day it took me and Earl-Dad from seven in the morning until six-thirty that night to find Boy, and when we finally returned home with him, we found LeDaire on the sofa with another man. Earl-Dad told the man to get out and then he forgave LeDaire, but I don't think she ever forgave him for forgiving her because she started the divorce proceedings and moved in with Lou almost immediately.

Lou was a big, strong man who owned an open-air market called Buddy's Place, where he sold a lot of beer and pork skins to local lawyers in the afternoon. They'd all come on over and hang out and tell stories about this case or that and they'd know that if their wife or girlfriend ever called looking for them, Lou would lie and say he hadn't seen them anywhere. It was their haven and Lou kept it that way. The only woman who was ever welcome at Buddy's Place was LeDaire. Any other woman who came in was usually a first and last date of a new lawyer, or else some woman just off the interstate looking for a Pepsi and some gum to keep her awake until she got to Florida or East Tennessee, because she surely wasn't going to be staying in Cordele, since no one else ever did. I am sure these women felt as uncomfortable walking out of that place as LeDaire felt comfortable walking in. She would dress herself up every day around four in her best slinky something and listen to those men tell dirty jokes until she didn't think she'd ever stop laughing. Lou would lean against the wall by the cash register, drinking a Budweiser, and smile to himself that he was just lucky enough to have landed himself a catch like her. I, myself, thought LeDaire had finally found herself a home she could be happy in for the rest of her life. I had thought Lou would be the perfect man for her to marry, even if I couldn't stand him. He was all love and attention for her. But it just goes to prove to you that a daughter does not know her mother, no matter what people think.

And I, myself, was thinking an awful lot as I sat at the Speeds' dinner table across from her and that horrid date she was with. It was like this. Daddy Speed was sitting right next to him, him and all those tattoos on his arms.

Well let me back up.

Buck had met me at the door, and after Sparkle had said, "Hey you creep," and kind of smiled at him and walked away, he had taken me into the backyard and said, "Dixie, what the hell were you doing with that guy last night?"

I had said, "Me? What about you and Sparkle? And don't think she didn't tell me everything, because she did."

He said, "Yeah, but all I did was kiss her. You were all over that guy."

Since it still wasn't clear what I'd done with Reno, and since I didn't know what to say, I simply said, "So. What's wrong with that. Unlike some people I know, he wants me to marry him." It had been a good lie.

Buck stopped dead in his tracks on that. He said, "Dixie, I see now that I've put you through too much stress not marrying you. I should never have asked you to leave like that. Would you reconsider what you're doing and come on back home where you belong? I really want you back girl. What do you say?"

So I had said, "Buck, it just hasn't worked out, this thing between you and me. So like I said, thanks, but no thanks."

"Dixie, I swear it'll be different this time. Trust me."

"Buck Speed, the only way I'll ever trust you again is if you put a ring on my finger and I've just walked down that wedding aisle."

"Well come on then. I'll call up Preacher Whatley tomorrow. And if I don't come through this time, you don't ever have to talk to me again. I'll leave you alone. Deal?"

It had a reasonable sound to me, so I gave in. "Deal."

It happened just like that, as fast as that. I was so happy. And by the time we had walked back to the front of the house to join Sparkle and the Speeds to tell them the good news, Momma and that horrid date of hers had arrived. And no one was talking to anyone. Daddy Speed was just standing in the doorway with a wrench dangling from his hand. Momma Speed was wringing her hands next to him. My own momma was playing with her date's ponytail. Besides all the tattoos, he had three earrings in one ear, one in the other, and he was sitting on the Speeds' couch with a beer in his hand. And he was smoking. And he wasn't saying much, thank God. And he was close to half Momma's age.

"Hey Dixie," said Momma, beaming when she saw me. "I want you to meet Johnny D. He plays the drums in a band. Isn't he the cutest thing," she said, flipping his ponytail again.

Johnny D. looked up at me and smiled. He said, "Hi babe."

I said, "LeDaire, can I see you for a minute. Out on the porch?"

Daddy Speed said in a low voice, "I think that's a good idea."

LeDaire said, "Oh, let's just all have dinner first and enjoy ourselves."

Daddy Speed shot me a hard dark look and Momma Speed didn't look up from her shoes. Buck squeezed my arm and whispered, "Dixie, is this some kind of joke?"

I hissed back, "You're the one who invited her."

Sparkle grabbed Buck's shoulder and whispered in his ear, "She probably met him through my mother. That's exactly the kind of man Momma likes to go out with."

"Well, they probably had a terrible fight over who was going to get him first," I said sarcastically.

At the dinner table Johnny D. said, "You got a beer in that fridge?"

Momma Speed smiled and said, "No. But I made a nice pitcher of sweet ice tea. Anyone want any tea?"

Daddy Speed said, "Yeah, Momma. Fill me up a glass," and he stared hard at Johnny D.'s ponytail.

Then, like right out of a nightmare, LeDaire started telling all these stories she'd learned from all those lawyers at Lou's place, up to and including the one about the black woman who rolled over in bed one night and subpoenaed her husband for a divorce, saying it was the only time she knew he'd be around to get the damned thing. And Daddy Speed had to interrupt her to say grace. And then LeDaire started telling another story about the naked, well-hung fat man who had died on the toilet and all the police who were surrounding him had to step aside to let a screaming woman through to get to him. And when they asked if she knew him, she stared at his big size and said, "No. But somebody sure lost a best friend."

And as if that wasn't bad enough, each time either LeDaire or Johnny D. took a trip to the bathroom, the other one would follow. And each time they'd come back necking more than the last, until at the end of the meal, which practically no one had eaten anyway, LeDaire was sitting on his lap, kissing up on his face, letting his hair out of his ponytail. It fell across his shoulders and Daddy Speed stood up, furious. He said, "That's about enough out of you two. I won't have this in my house. Dixie, you've gone too far this time. I want you and your mother out of here. Yall are nothing but white trash."

Momma Speed stood up and gasped. Buck stood up and looked like he was going to hit his daddy. Then he looked like he was going to hit me. Then he said, "Dixie, we'll talk about this another time. Get your momma and go on home now."

Daddy Speed, who wasn't finished with all he had to say, said, "I should have known when I saw those trashy pictures of you naked that you'd be trouble straight down the line."

LeDaire, who was way past drunk, laughed and said, "I beg your pardon. My daughter looked real good in those pictures."

I said, "Momma!"

Then Daddy Speed raised his hand like he was going to hit us all in one motion, but he stopped himself and said to LeDaire, "If you weren't a lady, I'd hit you so hard. Well, you ain't no lady, but you better get on out of here anyway."

He had a point there. I had to agree with him. LeDaire was no lady. But you either have to stand up for your own mother in this world, or you have to live for the rest of your life not doing it. One day she'd be an old woman and I'd try to explain to her that I'd never really hated her, that I'd just been scared of the things she'd done, because I hadn't wanted to end up doing the same things. And I'd hand her some crackers and she'd be thinking they were her shoe or an old photograph or something, because her memory would be all shot to hell. And I'd push her hair off her forehead and want to tell her that I'd turned out just like her anyway and it was a good thing too, because she'd been a real fireball, only it would be too late for her to understand. Well, standing there in front of the horrified Speeds, I realized that even though I didn't exactly feel that way now, I knew I'd feel that way later. It was one of those mysterious mother-daughter things, I guess, that made me realize that LeDaire wasn't so bad. She was just a passionate mess. And maybe she'd embarrassed everyone at the dinner table but she hadn't really hurt anyone.

So I said, "Come on, Momma. Let's you and me go on home. It's time to get you home."

She laughed and looked at Momma Speed, who was all tied up in a nice tight-knotted version of her old sweet self and said, "Loosen up, old girl. Haven't you ever been in love before?" And then she looked at Daddy Speed and burst out laughing.

I drove Johnny D.'s truck. Johnny D. sat in between me and LeDaire. He kept one of his hands on her lap the whole time, and half the time he kept trying to put his other one on mine. I was busy slapping him off, and when I wasn't, I was busy pulling over so LeDaire could throw up. Finally she just threw up in Johnny D.'s truck, and that's when he stopped trying to feel me off. He said, "Damn woman! What'd you go do that for?"

LeDaire just cracked up and threw up some more. She said, "Honey, I think we should stop off at the Tiger Alley for a nightcap."

I said, "Momma, you've had more than enough."

Johnny D. winked at me and said, "Let's just take her home," like, if I wanted him, he'd be free in about an hour. Gross, was what I thought.

Sparkle was following us in her car, so when I finally did drop them off at LeDaire's, I threw the keys at the back of Johnny D.'s head, and me and Sparkle took off for Donnie's.

His hot dog mobile was parked right out front where I wanted it to be. We knocked on the door, then walked right on in. First we had moved in without a moment's notice. Then we had left the same way. And now we were back and, not only was he happy to see us, he didn't ask word one about where we had been or what we had been doing or who we had been doing it with. No sirree. You could get a little peace around a guy like Donnie Sessions.

"Sparkle," I said. "Just sit there and watch TV. I'll be ready in a minute."

Donnie followed me out to my car, where some newer, cleaner clothes that showed a lot of leg waited for me. I had to get ready for Reno's talent scout friend. I was just hoping he was really going to show up. I needed a break bad!

Donnie said, "Dixie, baby," and stuck his hand right up my shirt.

I was looking in the backseat for my clothes, "Donnie, dammit, not now!"

He squeezed me tighter. "Oh come on, girl. You drive me crazy. How about just a little bit?"

"Nah, Donnie. I've got to be somewhere in twenty minutes. Where the hell did I put everything!"

"Doll baby, I only need ten. Come on, sugar. Ten's all it will take for me to show you around the world."

I laughed and pulled his hand away and said, "Donnie Sessions, you know what? I've missed you, you old son of a gun. But listen here," I said, turning around to face him. "I need just a little bit of time alone, okay? You understand?"

I really didn't want to hurt his feelings. He was looking at me like I'd shot his dog. Then slowly he cocked his head to the side and grinned that grin of his that got us together in the first place and said, "Dixie, for you, anything." Then he left me there to go through all my stuff.

Nearly everything was wrinkled, and not just unfolded wrinkled, but like someone had come along and wet it all up and wringed it out and jammed it into a small corner. And with my fake rabbit fur coat on, I was getting mighty hot going through it all. So I took off the jacket, and took off the sequined tube top, and after what seemed like weeks of wearing that thing, I'm here to tell you it felt good taking it off. The whole area of skin that had been under all that elastic was now puckered, but finally breathing. I just sat on the passenger side of my old Dodge Charger—the yellow one that Buck had been promising to paint metallic blue all summer long—and I knew now that it would never be painted blue, and I rubbed my skin and cried and cried and cried. I put my head on the dashboard, next to the big crack with the foam coming out, and cried some more. I cried for me and Buck, mostly. I cried for Momma Speed, remembering her hugging me before I left, and Daddy Speed pulling her away, saying, "Get away from her." I cried for her Visa card, and for the Waikiki–Myrtle Beach Hotel that was charging yet another night on the bill. I cried because I'd lost the tight jeans contest, and because no matter how hard I tried, I'd never be able to come up with the money to pay Buck's momma back, or to pay for my modeling school fee. I lifted my head and looked up at Donnie's trailer and then I really started crying. The lights in his place never looked quite as bright as lights coming from a real house. They were dim, like I imagined the 1940s were, and I just couldn't see living in dim. I needed real brightness. So I cried some more. I cried for Reno and Jerry, who were real nobodies trying to be real somebodies, and they looked like all the future I was ever going to have. And then I cried because Daddy Speed had given Sparkle a hug before he had kicked me out, and Buck had seen it, and I just never understood how come Buck or his daddy had never seen the naked pictures of Sparkle, just of me, and how come they didn't have to see Sparkle's trampy momma, Trina, but they had to see mine, and how come all my fucking clothes were wrinkled and I was broke and my whole damn world was falling apart and Sparkle was just sitting in that stupid trailer watching TV, unaffected by the whole thing.

A palmetto bug flew in the window and hit the dashboard and then my face. "Ahhh!" I screamed, swatting it away, and that's when something sharp poked my side. I reached down and tried to pull it out, but it was jammed in under the seat. So I turned on the inside light of my car and worked it out and then there it was. It was like the lollipop on top of the whole bad present of my life—the box of letters that Paulette had sent to Buck, and Buck had saved, and I had never read, but had always wanted to. It was the only thing in my whole car, my whole life, that was in order, with a shiny blue satin ribbon holding it shut. I snapped the ribbon open, whipped off the top of the box, and the smell of perfume came wafting up at me. It smelled so nice. It made me jealous, but it was okay. Just holding these things of Paulette's made me closer to Buck. I couldn't wait to read the letters, to see what she was really like. I'd wanted to read them for so long but I'd never felt safe enough to. But sitting there in my car, with no chance in hell of Buck showing up, I was safe now. The first one read:

Dear Honey-Bean,

I'm flying to a different town every day. It's a wonder I don't go crazy missing you. But my life is so full of new adventures. As I write this, we are about to land in Dallas. Imagine Dallas! Home of the Cowboys! Today I was in charge of first class for the first time! We flew out of Kennedy Airport, New York! (New York is sooo cool!) Most of my customers are businessmen. After I pour them all champagne, there's a little time left to talk to them. Today I met a photographer!!! who has actually done lots of famous models!!!! He wants to photograph me! He knows an agent I can call! He gave me the number, so I'm going to call tomorrow. Well, with all this happening, it's hard to think of anything else. What excitement! I miss you. Gotta go! We're about to touchdown!!!

Love ya!

Your sunny girl, Paulette

Yuk. She had drawn hearts all over the letter. She had dotted all her *i*'s with smiley faces. Practically every sentence ended with an exclamation mark.

I read another one. Then I read a few more. They all said the same thing. They all smelled the same way. I couldn't place the perfume. Wind Song? Wild Musk? Tatiana? Scoundrel? I couldn't place it. It sort of smelled like the cheap cosmetic counter at the Kroger Supermarket, not the expensive lineup at Newberry's Department Store where I, myself, bought Elizabeth Taylor's Passion.

I must have read twenty of those cheap-smelling letters sitting there in my hot car. I wanted to jump ahead to the last ones, the ones that had been postdated the last month I had lived with Buck, to see if she'd written anything about me. But I didn't want to ruin the pace. I wanted to read them in the exact order Buck had read them so I could get a clue as to a buildup or a letdown between them.

But I'd have to wait. I was running out of time. She wasn't the only one who had a date with a hot ticket to New York City. Me and Sparkle had to get cracking if we wanted to make it to our talent scout in time. Reno better not have been lying, was all I could say. One way or another, Reno or no Reno, I was going to make it to New York City and get out of this small-fry town and show them all.

26

So where is he?" I asked Reno when we walked into the Tiger Alley Saloon.

He said, "He'll be here. Just hold your horses."

Sparkle said flatly, "Forget him. Where's that honey-pie, Jerry? I sure don't want to go a whole evening without seeing him."

"Don't worry doll baby," said Jerry, coming up and leaning over the table, kissing her on the cheek. "I'm here and raring to go."

She rubbed his kiss off. "Whoopie dee do."

It was about thirty minutes until the midnight show began and the crowd was pretty thin for eleven-thirty. The cocktail waitress came over, dressed in a short tiger-printed Danskin outfit, with a tiger tail dragging behind. She said, "Usual?"

Reno smiled at her like an old friend. "Yeah honey. And listen, bring a couple martinis for our girls here."

"Wait," I said, "make that a beer. I've still got a hangover."

Reno said, "Make it a martini."

"But I don't want a martini," I said through my teeth after the waitress winked at him and walked away.

"Yeah you do," he said, smiling, taking my hand under the table. I looked at him hard. That nose, those lips, the way his eyes were too close together—I hadn't really kissed him, had I? Surely I hadn't done anything else with him. Surely, even drunk, I wouldn't lose my sense of taste?

Sparkle was still fighting off Jerry. "Look, keep your greasy paws to yourself," she said.

"I didn't touch you." He laughed. "Look, my hands are right up here on the table. When did I touch you?"

"Every time you move you run your leg up against mine."

"Well," said Jerry, ignoring her, leaning over to me. "Well, well, well, well, well. What we've got here is two classy broads wanting to break into the modeling world, huh?"

I rolled my eyes. "My, my, you do catch on fast, don't you?"

Sparkle rolled her eyes at Reno. "So what do we have to do here to hook up with this talent guy? Put up with this lady-killer all night long?"

Reno said, "I told you to hang on. He'll be here." He checked his watch. "He wants to see what you two look like onstage. He won't be able to sign you on until he does."

I jerked my hand away from his. "Wait a minute now. You didn't say anything about going up onstage."

"Well baby," Reno said, grabbing my hand again. "It's like this. You girls don't have a portfolio, so you've got to show him something. Just enter this contest, he'll see your stuff and you'll be on that next plane for New York City. I'll bet you big money."

"Wait," I said. "What's the show tonight anyway? It isn't a nudie or anything, is it? I'm not doing a nudie."

Jerry snorted and Reno squeezed my hand. "No hon. I wouldn't have you do that."

"Sure," said Sparkle.

"Look," he said, "I'm not really sure what it is. But does it matter? What matters is, he sees how you gals work an audience. Think you can handle it?"

"It depends on whether yall are the judges or not," said Sparkle. "If you remember correctly, you shortchanged me last night."

The waitress came over with our drinks and interrupted, "All right, sugar pies, are they entering or not? The manager's got to know."

Me and Sparkle looked at each other. "Hey," I said. "I don't think I like you entering us before we even give our permission. That's real crap."

Reno said, "Calm down. We had to hold a spot open for you." He was beginning to look mad. "I've gone to a lot of trouble to set this up. You going to do it, or what?"

"What kind of contest is this?" I asked the waitress.

But Reno interrupted. "Look girls, it's no sweat off my back if you don't do it. But come on, Dixie. It's just a stupid contest. Besides, there's a five-hundred-dollar first prize. I don't see how you can lose. Now go on. This guy's going to be here any minute and I want to make sure he sees you in the best possible light."

In the backroom, the manager gave all the girls T-shirts with the Tiger Alley Saloon logo printed across the front, way up near the neckline, far above where a normal printing usually goes. He pointed to the same leather skirt I'd been wearing about forty days straight and said, "You sure you want to wear that thing? Here, I'll give you a pair of shorts. I'll give you both a pair of shorts. I don't think you want to get those clothes wet."

"Wet?" I asked. "What's this contest all about, anyway?"

He looked at me like I was crazy and threw the shorts at me. "Go on. Hurry up. The show's about to start. What kind of contest is this," he muttered, walking away, shaking his head. All the girls around him laughed.

"Dixie," said Sparkle under her breath.

"I don't know, Sparkle. Don't ask me anything."

You know, you hear the words "New York talent scout" and you want to believe. You want to know this means serious business. You want to know it means a Park Avenue suite with limos and good looking men and a full life. So it didn't even occur to me, I don't know about Sparkle, but it just damned well did not occur to me that we'd be up on a stage entering a sleazy wet T-shirt contest.

But there we were. One by one, we all stepped up on the runway, and one by one we stepped into the blue kiddie pool in the center of that runway and Charlie Enlow, from the night before, wetted us down with a hose. This time we didn't have fake names or a paper bag over our heads. This time we didn't need any of that. Believe you me I thought about heading out of there before I did it, but like I said, there are just some things I can't account for and one of them was me standing in that kiddie pool like the rest of those idiot girls. Charlie sprayed me down. I tried to look out to where Reno was. I was going to tell him a thing or two when it was all over. But the lights were much brighter than the night before. I just couldn't see anything but the other girls onstage. God, I was embarrassed. And it's not like I had the biggest breasts in the world either. And with that cold, cold water splashing on them, making them smaller and tighter, I felt like a boy. I kept thinking of the five-hundred-dollar prize and the talent scout and all those men looking at my nipples. And suddenly, out of all the girls onstage lining up for their turn at the kiddie pool, I see a very, very angry Casey. Casey from Renee's World of Modeling, Casey who had been kicked out of there. Her eyes were blazing at me. I knew she was going to tell on me. I knew it like I knew I wasn't going to win. It's like any of my boyfriends have always said to me every time I've even asked them if they thought I was too small. They'd always smile and say, "Dixie, you've got the perfect size. You can fit them in a wineglass, perfectly."

Maybe. But something told me you needed a little more than a wineglass up top to win a five-hundred-dollar wet T-shirt contest.

☆

I do not think Buck will ever become a televangelist. He does not have that kind of crazy energy. No, a slower energy burns behind those eyes. He is not able to see the whole scheme of things. This is why he makes a good bodybuilder. He can focus on one muscle connected to one heavy weight, lifting, lowering, straining, breathing. I used to hate watching him lift. I'd go crazy with the boredom. You see, I do have the popping energy it takes to be a televangelist. So sitting there, watching Buck lift, would physically hurt my head. The inside of my brain would be zapping around making me clamp my teeth and tighten my lips until I'd be ready to scream. And he'd turn to me proudly and say, "How many was that, Dixie? Were you counting?"

I never was. So I'd say, "Buck, I think that was ten. But I'm not sure."

He'd look real disappointed and say, "But sweetheart, you told me you'd count for me."

I'd roll my eyes at him and say, "Okay, okay, it was ten. Yes, I'm sure it was. I remember now."

Then he'd grin and pick up another weight for another ten reps of some other muscle group. It just about drove me nuts.

Well, now I miss watching him oiling down his body and posing in front of the mirror for long periods of time. I miss that sweating excitement that would take over him when he'd have a good workout. When he'd come over to me with his eyes shining and kiss me and say, "Dixie, me and you make a good team. Someday we're going to have five little bodybuilders running around our ankles."

I'd look at my thin ankles and remember what LeDaire always said about ankles and having babies. But I wanted those five little weight lifters. My feet could swell up to full bloat for all I cared. I'd just get Buck to teach me a thing or two on his Nautilus machine. With my good looks and him looking so good, we'd be a handsome family.

Buck would get real quiet after his workouts. He'd go take a seat in front of his TV and turn it on without really watching. He'd be daydreaming. Without being able to see the full scheme of things, he was scheming up his future. He saw it as one straight line of the right thing to do. Plan A leads to plan B leads to plans C, D, E, F, G and on to Z. It was just that way with Buck. Those were the times I'd get scared, because the way I worked, you could never tell what letter I was going to hit up on. I saw my future as one great big zigzaggy line of doing all the wrong things. And I'd watch old Buck sitting there daydreaming and think, "He must be trying to figure out how I fit in with his straight line." The answer was, I was never going to fit.

This is what I was thinking about as Reno handed me and

Sparkle each a ten-dollar bill for losing the wet T-shirt contest. I was furious. Sparkle wasn't happy either. She crumpled up the bill and threw it at his face. "Okay buster. What is this?"

Reno said, "Sorry gals. Looks like you didn't make the cut again."

Jerry wrapped his arm around Sparkle and looked down at her T-shirt. "Ummm-ummm baby, if I'd have been the judge, that five hundred bucks would be yours for the asking."

Sparkle pulled away and crossed her arms over her chest. She was like me. She couldn't believe she'd done it, and she couldn't believe she'd lost, either.

"Well where's the big-time talent scout?" I asked.

"Dixie," Reno said, "listen. He didn't show. I'm sorry. I don't know what to say."

So I said, "Sparkle, he doesn't know anybody. The sooner we figure that out the better we'll be."

It seemed like we stood there for a very long time. Me and Sparkle looking at Reno. Reno looking at me. Jerry looking at Sparkle's and my chests.

Then I turned on Reno like a snake. "You know, I've had just about enough out of you, mister," I hissed. "You did this just to go out with me, didn't you? Why you creep. What's a matter? Didn't get enough last night?" I was boiling mad.

Reno huffed, "Get enough. We didn't get anything. You girls act like you're guarding a treasure chest or something. We've got a name for you. Up north we call you prick teasers. Go on. Run on home to your boyfriends where you belong."

Whoever thought I'd be that happy entering and losing a slutty contest like that. Whoever thought I'd feel so clean! It was worth it just to find out I hadn't done anything. So me and Sparkle stormed out of there, laughing and hugging each other and freezing to death, because once you've been up onstage getting your T-shirt sprayed down with ice cold water, it seems like forever before you can get warm enough again.

27

You know, there are a lot of what-ifs out there. Like, what if Casey had called Renee and told her about me and Sparkle? What if Renee had called us and kicked us out of modeling school? What if Sparkle had decided to run off with Donnie Sessions in his old hot dog mobile, thereby leaving me all by myself to come up with all the money I owed? Or what if this or what if that? Well, just don't let some old wise man come along and tell you that you'd be better off not worrying about the what-ifs in the world. Because I am here to tell you, they can happen.

Me and Sparkle were back at the Waikiki–Myrtle Beach Hotel in a double suite with a Jacuzzi, and we were in that Jacuzzi trying to figure out a way to come up with some money to pay off our bill, when we got the call.

"Hello," I said, gathering up some bubbles around me.

"Is this Dixie?"

"Yes, it is," I said. "Who is this?" It was late.

"This is Renee."

She didn't sound too good. As a matter of fact, she sounded real, real bad. She said, "Well it didn't take you long, did it? Frankly, I'm just as disappointed as I can be."

"What?" I said. Then I knew. One o'clock in the morning explained it all.

"Listen honey," she said. "You may play me for a fool, but I'm not stupid. Don't even think about coming back to my school in your lifetime."

"Renee!" I said, sitting up, splashing water everywhere. Sparkle sat up straighter too and mouthed the word "What?"

"And one more thing," Renee went on. "Why don't you do your friend, Sparkle, a favor and don't go getting her involved in all your trash. She has a real shot at a modeling career if you'll just leave her alone."

"Hold on a minute, Renee," I said, but she had already hung up.

"Sparkle, the worst thing has happened. You're not going to believe it. Renee found out about the contest. Shit. Shit." I got out of the Jacuzzi, dripping bubbles all the way to the towel rack. "Shit! What am I going to do?"

"What about me?" asked Sparkle.

"She didn't find out about you. The only thing she said about you was I should leave you alone, that I was a bad influence on you. Damn. Imagine that." I wrapped a towel around my hair like a turban and grabbed another one for my waist.

"You know, I'm getting sick of this," Sparkle said. She turned the water on to make it hotter and added more bubble bath in with it. "I mean, I'm sick and tired of never being noticed. It wasn't like I wasn't up on that stage with you. It's always Dixie this and Dixie that."

"Sparkle!"

"Well," she said, "I can't help it. I mean, it's good I didn't get in trouble and all, but still, I'm just as pretty as you are. I could at least get noticed." She was mad. She was going off into a sulk. It didn't make any sense. I was the one hurting. It was like telling a man that you'd just caught him going out with another woman behind your back and him turning around and telling you that you were a real creep for spying on him.

"Don't get mad at me," I shouted. "If anyone should be mad around here, it should be me! It was your idea to do those stupid contests in the first place. How come you're always getting let off the hook anyway? Huh, answer me that one."

"Fuck off," she said, going completely under the water. When she came back up, I was toweling off, furious. Not much could come between me and Sparkle, we were such good friends, so when something did happen, it usually took a long time to patch things up. It worried me. Mad and worried at someone is a hard combination. I had to count on her for helping me out of the mess I was in and at the same time I wanted to tell her to fuck off right back to her face. Instead I put baby powder on my shoulders and concentrated on not saying a word.

Sparkle rose out of her bubbles and looked at me real hard. Then she said, "Dixie, have you taken a good look at your boobs lately? They've gotten huge!"

"Oh shut up, Sparkle."

"No, really. They're like basketballs compared to what they used to be."

I looked in the mirror. There they were. The first real boobs I'd ever had. I had noticed them the night before, when I was running in the store to pick up some food for me and Donnie. They'd pulled the skin on my neck down when they bounced. It had been the strangest feeling. And then at the wet T-shirt contest, I'd looked down expecting to see flat-chested, but instead what I saw was sticking out proudly. I hadn't been able to account for where they had come from. Maybe Buck had been right when he said I was putting on weight. Maybe it was true what they said about daughters turning into their mothers. LeDaire had started out skinny, but her body ended up looking just like Grandmother Maybelle's, who never was fat, but she wasn't skinny either. She was just kind of blocky. Maybe I was turning into Grandmother Maybelle, too. That would be the worst thing. There was no such thing as a famous blocky model.

Well if it was true, there wasn't much time left in this old body. I had to get cracking. I had to make the most of what was left of my good years. I sat down on the floor next to the Jacuzzi and, with the adrenaline that shoots through a woman the first time she realizes she's getting fat, I did seventy-five hard sit-ups. A one, breathe, and a two, breathe, and a three, breathe, and a why in the hell did Casey have to go and tell on me, four, five, six, seven, eight, breathe. And by the time I got to seventy-five, I was ready.

"Where are you going?" Sparkle asked, drying off.

"I'm going to find that bitch, Casey," I said.

"But Dixie, we can't go out now. I'm tired."

So I said, "Just stay put. I'll be back in a little bit."

☆

Casey was still at the Tiger Alley. She was sitting on a bar stool, drinking a beer. It was late. Last call for alcohol had been announced an hour ago. The lights had brightened and the jukebox plug was pulled out.

"So how's the little model doing?" she asked. She didn't seem surprised to see me.

"What's the big idea, Casey?" I said, knocking her shoulder with my fist. "I don't even know you."

"What?" She studied me hard. "Wait a minute, sister, I don't exactly know you either." She stood up. "If you want to know the truth, bitch, I don't even know your name. What happened, Renee find out you're a tramp or something?"

I just stared at her. It was only a matter of seconds before I dragged her outside.

"Listen here," she said, loosening up. "She's got these secret little elves that seem to have the inside scoop on all of us. I swear, I didn't tell her a thing."

So I said, "Yeah, well who the hell did then? And if you didn't tell, how'd you know she knew?"

"Oh honey," said Casey, "it's written all over your face. Hey, you want to know something funny? I was the one that told on myself."

I was floored. "You told on your own self?"

Casey reached over the bar and pulled a couple of beers waiting to be stocked off the sink. "Here," she said. "You see, Renee had me in this skintight contract where I paid her twenty-five percent of anything I made, and I wasn't exactly making enough to do that. So then I run across this other agency, they're out of Charlotte, but still, they said they'd only take ten percent off the top. So, I knew the only way to get loose from her claws was to let her think I'd gone bad. If Renee had even thought someone was after me, she'd never have let me out of my contract. This way, she just tore it up right in front of my face. You know, you can make a hell of a lot more money doing the contest circuit than you ever can modeling in this hick town."

I couldn't believe my ears. Renee was the greatest modeling teacher in the South. Anyone with brains could see she'd trained the most beautiful women in the world. If she wanted twenty-five percent, maybe it was because she earned that much. I said, "Casey, what about what Renee did for Vanna White? You're so beautiful. She could have gotten you discovered if you'd just given her some time."

"Ha!" She leaned back on her stool and grabbed her ears. "I can't believe what I'm hearing. You mean you actually bought that crap? You actually believed that story about her discovering Vanna White? Ha! That's great. You know what? Renee met Vanna White once when Vanna was doing a spot at the Briarcliffe Mall. And Vanna said something to her about how much she liked the way Renee wore her eye shadow and Renee told her how to do it and Vanna said she'd try it sometime and ever since then, Renee's been going around saying she discovered her. Now isn't that some shit."

My ears were ringing. I finished off my beer and reached across the bar for Casey's.

"And you know what?" Casey said.

"No, what?" I was getting sick.

"I'm not even sure she really met her. Sometimes I think she made that up, too." Casey kind of laughed quietly to herself, then she looked at me concerned. "Hey, you're really upset about this, aren't you?"

"Yeah. I wanted to be a model. I've lost my boyfriend and I figured the only way to get him back was to become famous." I started biting my fingernail and Casey reached over and pulled my hand away. "Well, you probably don't need Renee for that. Something tells me the most famous models in the world never even went to modeling school. Hey, that friend of yours, what's her name?"

"Sparkle?"

"She the one in here with you tonight?"

"Yeah," I said.

"Did Renee kick her out, too?"

"No. That's the weird thing about Sparkle. She never gets in any trouble."

"Well, that figures." Casey took both my hands and looked me straight in the eye. "You know, Dixie, if I were you, I'd think on that one for a while. After all, it seems to me that she was the only one here that knew you."

☆

I would be just so glad to have somebody that loved me and everything. A husband. But since I couldn't have that, the next best thing was to be a model. I have said this once and I'll say it again. To be a model would be to be beautiful, clean, pure. I wanted to walk down those high-fashion runways with everyone looking up at me wanting to be me, instead of me being stuck in these crummy small towns hating being me.

I wanted to be better than anyone I knew. I wanted to hold my head up until my neck felt so good from doing it. I could stretch my head so high and twist it around while it was up there and just feel what it would be like.

I wasn't stupid. I knew models had problems. But I knew that no matter what those problems were, they weren't as lonely and closed in as the problems of a small town girl. A high-fashion model could put her problems on a leash and walk them around town. Me, my problems crushed my sides in, like a mean father grabbing your arms and shaking all the good stuff loose from you until there was nothing left but the scary bad.

Casey said Renee would never take me back.

☆

I have got to stop hanging around Sparkle. She is the trickiest person I know. There is a slyness about her that winds around my uneasiness until I do not know what has hit me.

Like BOOM! I'm caught posing nude, and BOOM! I'm caught entering sleazy contests, and *whispppppp*, she breezes out of this trouble like it has not touched her, instead of her being the one to start it all up in the first place.

Normally, I can tell somebody to screw off. But there was never any evidence of wrongdoing with old Sparkle.

For instance, I got back to the hotel and there she was, sleeping like a baby. Her face looked so soft and sweet with her hair flowing out around her pillow until I felt like hugging her all up in my arms, when before I just felt like coming in and murdering her. Her fist was balled up near her cheek like she was about to suck her thumb and she was breathing, almost snoring, sounding like a baby lamb might sound standing near its momma.

I sat down in a chair beside her and stared at her face. I whispered, "Sparkle?"

She did not move.

I whispered, "Sparkle, are you awake?"

She moved just enough for me to know it was the real thing. She was not faking.

So I just sat and waited. I didn't know what it was I was waiting for. For something to hit me out of the clear blue, I guess, to tell me what to do.

She moved. I whispered, "Sparkle, that air force guy is on the phone, Roy. Want to talk to him?" Nothing. No movement on that, she was surely asleep. So I did what they do in the movies. I thought it would work. It was supposed to act like a truth serum. You whispered questions in a person's ear while they slept, and they'd talk. So I whispered, "Sparkle, have you tried to do anything bad to Dixie Riggs?" Still nothing. Well something. She breathed a little deeper.

So I said, "Sparkle, did you do anything bad to Dixie?" Nothing. I got off the chair and crept quietly over to her. I whispered deep in her ear, "Sparkle, you were bad to Dixie Riggs, weren't you?"

She bolted up, startled, swatting at her head. "What's up? What's going on?"

"Nothing," I said, disappointed. I thought for sure she'd

spill all her bad beans so I could start hating her without a doubt.

"Dixie, are you okay?" She rubbed her eyes like a little girl and got out of bed. She was so tall, so skinny. She loomed four inches taller than me. Those four inches sealed my fate. Because of them, she'd make it. I would not. She'd be able to buy two-thousand-dollar gloves, go to cool rock and roll bars with good looking French clothes designers, and dance the nights away with exotic Russian male ballet stars. She'd be able to hop from plane to plane to country to country and have a perfume named after her. I could see it now. Sparkle Starling, high-fashion model. And there I'd be, Dixie Riggs, nobody. Dixie Riggs, four inches shorter than Sparkle. Four inches was shorter than my comb, shorter than a candy bar, shorter than Daddy Speed's sideburns. Four inches was shorter than my dream.

"Dixie, why you looking so sad, girl? Is everything all right?" Sparkle mussed up my hair, the way Buck always did when he didn't want to make love.

I examined her face. Her hair could throw you off. You could see all that long blond hair swinging as she walked and not notice that she didn't have a lick of looks. Her nose was too big. Her face was too flat. Her cheeks were too wide. Her teeth were too yellow. But those could be fixed. Would that make a difference, I had to ask myself? "Sparkle, come here. Let's try something."

"What?"

I know it sounds disgusting, but it isn't, really. All you have to do is go down to the store and pick up the supplies. Then, you take a Brillo pad and scrub your teeth with it. After that, you dip a Q-tip in a capful of Clorox, then hold the end of it on each individual tooth, thereby letting it soak in, and ZOWEE! your teeth will look just as good as they do after you leave the dentist!

"I don't like this. Are you sure you know what you're doing?" It was about an hour later and Sparkle was standing in the bathroom, stamping her feet as I filed her teeth with an emery board. The 7-Eleven was all out of Brillo pads.

"Just hold still," I said. I grabbed her jaw tighter. "I can't do this unless you hold still. Gosh, you're touchy." Gosh, her teeth were dirty. "Sparkle, when was the last time you ever went to see a dentist? No. Don't answer."

The filing part took the better part of ten minutes. The Clorox part took forever. Sparkle kept pulling her head away, sticking her tongue out, going, "Ooooo! I hate this."

"Sparkle, if you'd just keep still, it wouldn't drip in your mouth so much."

Anyway, when it was all over, Sparkle's teeth gleamed as bright as the Waikiki-Myrtle porcelain sink. She wiped away her tears and we both stared at each other in the mirror.

"Gee, Dix. They've never been this white."

"Okay, but don't go doing this all the time. I wouldn't do it more than once or twice a month."

"I look gorgeous." She lifted her lip up with her finger and stuck her teeth right up to the mirror.

"Sparkle, do you think about modeling like I do? I mean, do you dream about it all the time?" I hitched myself up on the sink counter and crossed my legs.

"Nah. Yeah, well, sometimes."

"Oh." I leaned back on the mirror. She looked so pretty now, big nose or not.

"Why?"

"Oh, I was just wondering. Hey Spark, you didn't tell Renee on me, did you?"

"Oh Dixie!" she said. She turned to me with her mouth wide open. "How could you? I can't believe you'd even think that." She stomped off and got in bed, taking up the whole mattress. It was easy to see that she was hinting for me to leave her alone.

"Sparkle," I said.

"No. Don't even try to apologize." She pulled the covers over her head.

"I wasn't. I just wanted to know how Renee knew we were here?"

☆

About those what-ifs. They can happen. They can just move right on in and make a whole career out of your life. There

I was, asleep one minute, hearing the hotel door slamming the next. I was disoriented at first. I walked around the suite. There was no sign of Sparkle. Then I found the note Scotch-taped to the bathroom mirror, right above the Clorox bottle. It read:

> *Dear Dix,*
> *Sorry girl, but I need to take a break from you. I'm not sure you're thinking right. Donnie said I could move back in with him. Your car is parked in the hotel parking lot. He drove it over. Sorry, but I think it's better this way.*
> *Love, Sparkle*

She had written the note with my new World of Modeling black eyeliner pencil. The tip was smushed, laying in a glob of toothpaste in the sink. And she had taped my car keys to the faucet, which was leaking on the eye pencil. After going around the room, looking in the closet and under the beds, one of my worst suspicions had come true. My fake rabbit fur coat, the one Sparkle had been eyeing ever since I'd bought it, was gone.

The clock on the TV said three A.M. It was hard to imagine that two hours ago Renee had called and kicked me out; that an hour ago I'd had a beer with Casey; that thirty minutes ago Sparkle and I were laughing it up; and now I was all alone. So much had gone on in such a short time. Who had shown Buck the pictures? Who had told Renee about me? Why had Sparkle left? I didn't want to connect all those questions and come up with the one answer that made any sense. My stomach felt strange. Everything was wrong.

28

I walked out to the beach. The Myrtle Beach moon was way over in the far left-hand corner of the ocean, making a long white trail across the water to me. Little green phosphorescent somethings popped up around my feet when I kicked the sand. In front of me and behind me, a dirty looking foam that looked like it came out of a Laundromat stuck to the shore, close to the water, but not touching it. I took off my shoes and waded. The waves came up, the waves went back, just like how Buck came into my life and left, and came in and left. The only thing constant were the little sand crabs that were always there after the water left, trying to dig themselves into the sand again. I felt just like them. Every time he left, I felt like I was trying to dig into the sand again. Only it felt like mud to me, real dirt. And my boobs were big, just like Sparkle said. It felt like the full moon was pulling them like it was pulling the high tide. Then it came to me. I was pregnant. I didn't have a job. I didn't have any health insurance. I wasn't married. And those six short short weeks to being a high-fashion model were turning into six long stretched-out ones of being nothing. Lord. I was pregnant.

People always think bodybuilders are so dumb. They see them walking down the road shooting their pecs, and they get the wrong idea. They see them oiling their big chests down, flexing their muscles in the sun, walking with their arms away from their bodies like they're about to start flapping their wings for takeoff. They watch them walk through the A&P aisles with their feet spread wide because their thighs aren't able to touch any longer. Most people see bodybuilders as types who can't pull anything over their heads but stretch T-shirts, who haven't read a book since *Frog and Toad* and who never ever think about anyone but themselves because they're too busy studying their own bodies to know what's going on in the human mind of anyone else. Well, I am here to tell you this isn't always true.

There I was, walking along feeling sorry for myself one minute, and the next minute I see Buck Speed's shadow in the moonlight. The reason I know it's Buck is because, yes, his arms do look like they're about to take off, and because he's carrying a book. You see, Buck reads two books a day sometimes. And somewhere in that beefy body of his is a homing device that leads to me whenever I'm truly in trouble. He knows. He may be thinking of his body, but he's busy thinking about my mind. He may not have known I was trying to figure out if this was his baby or Donnie Sessions's baby, or that I was even filled up with a baby, but he did know I was in big, big trouble.

He said, "Well, hey there, stranger," as if we always bumped into each other on the beach, five miles from home, at three in the morning.

I said, "Oh Buck."

He said, "I know, baby. I know."

"Buck. I'm so sorry about my momma. She's a real mess. I'm so sorry."

And Buck, being the sport he is, said, "She's just fine. I liked her just fine. Daddy'll get over it. Deep down he really loves you Dixie."

I said, "Buck, the whole world is crashing down on me. I feel like walking into the ocean and never coming back."

He put his arm around me, his big bodybuilding arm, and said, "Well, we wouldn't want you doing that now, would we?"

I started crying. It's so weird. The minute someone's nice to you, it always feels like it'll be okay to spill your guts and tell them the whole story. Buck took off his linen jacket and spread it across the sand and sat me down. I almost started in with the "I don't know whose baby it is, but it could be so and so's, or it could be so and so's, or it could be yours, but that doesn't matter, because what's really pressing me right now is the fact that I've got this room up there for the third night at the Waikiki-Myrtle that's being charged up on your momma's Visa, and you don't mind, do you? You'll take care of all this, won't you?"

What a relief it would have been to toss it all out like that. But even me, Dixie Riggs, is not that stupid. So I just sat on his jacket and leaned against his chest and felt my head rise up and down to the rhythm of his breathing. I picked up a broken shell with my toes and dropped it back in the sand. Then I picked it up again and dropped it again. Buck didn't move.

We sat there for a long, long time not saying a word. The white lighted lane that the moon had made across the ocean had now turned into a yellow trickle of light, and somewhere off in the distance I could hear a sea turtle making a mad dash for the water. Buck had taught me about turtles a long time ago, about how they came to the same place where they were born to bury their eggs, and I tried to imagine going home to Cordele to get married and have my baby there, and I couldn't. What a sorry lot for a child that would be.

"Oh Buck," I sighed.

"What is it, baby?"

"Buck, I'm having real problems here."

Then he said, "Let's not talk about them now. They won't look so bad tomorrow. Just come here and let me kiss you."

So me and Buck kissed and kissed. We kissed while the moon finished going down and we kissed until the blues and pinks of the morning began lighting up the sky. Then we went up to suite 501 at the Waikiki-Myrtle where we could kiss some more, but instead Buck took a step back and said, "Damn Dixie! Where'd you get the money to pay for all this?"

I said, "Oh, it didn't cost anything. It looks more expensive than it is."

He went over to the Jacuzzi and turned it on. It made a wild sucking noise into the air, looking for water. He turned it off. "Dixie," he said. "What's up?"

So I said, "Honest, Buck. Nothing. I did a few modeling gigs here and this was the only room available so they gave it to me." I tacked on, "You see, I did a couple a bathing suit pictures for their new summer brochure." He seemed to believe me, so I tacked on more. "Tomorrow night I'm doing a dinner scene in their dining room that they're going to hang up in the elevator along with the dinner menu. You know, it's just business."

"Wow, you're really doing well, aren't you?" He looked sad. A reaction out of my stony Buck Speed!

I started lying more. I said, "Yeah, and not only that, but they're sending down a famous male model from New York City, one of those guys with the long hair, and he's going to be in the picture with me. We get to have lobster and champagne and any old thing we want. And after that, we're going on a midnight cruise. You know, it's fun and all," I said, watching Buck being fascinated, "but you can really get tired hanging around all those bright lights all day. And this ocean breeze is a terror on my hair."

People always go around saying such stupid things like, "If you lie, you're just spinning yourself into a web you'll never get out of," or, "You can never trust a liar," or, "If you lie, you have to pay for the consequences and those consequences can never lead to any good." Well lying has always taken a bad rap, but I'll always trust a liar over someone who can't lie at all, unless of course they lie about something really stupid. But a creative liar is one of the best people you'll ever meet. And as far as paying for consequences goes, well, if I sat down with Buck Speed in that Jacuzzi and told him the truth, it would not set me free. I know this way of thinking was all messed up, that it barely made a lick of sense, but it was good enough reasoning for me. And the most important thing was, Buck believed me. After all, when it all boiled down to it, it was my intentions that mattered and my intentions were all focused on me loving Buck. You can't get on a girl for intentions like that. And like I said, if I'd told the truth, we would never have gotten into that Jacuzzi or that big bed and this way I got both and my Buck back and who could ask for anything more? I ask you?

One thing Preacher Whatley doesn't seem to understand is that God is always on standby for sinners like me. He is like a doctor with a beeper. I go through these terrible mazes of hell by myself, and finally, when I can't find my way out, I yell, "Oh God, please come help me. I can't do it alone anymore," and there it goes, the beeper, letting Him know I need Him, and letting me know He was there the whole time. I mean, okay with the "If you sin, you're going to hell" bit, but somewhere out there is a little bitty gray area that Jesus allows for poor old messed-up fools like me to work in.

I was in that gray area now. And Jesus was standing by, making sure I didn't mess things up too bad. I mean, okay, I'd already made a mess. But Jesus wasn't going to let me go over the edge. That's all I'm trying to say. And when I was out there on that beach, out in the moonlight, pregnant like the loggerhead sea turtles coming in to lay their eggs, crying for help, I think Jesus sent me Buck. I know you can't guess what God's plans are for you, but somehow I was convinced that Buck was a special agent from heaven, sent down to set me straight.

We spent three days together. Three lovely and gorgeous days where we talked about marriage and children. Buck said, "I want you wearing the prettiest whitest dress you can find. And then we're going to Acapulco for our honeymoon. Would you like that? Acapulco?"

"I'd like going anywhere with you, Buck."

"And we'll get you pregnant right away. Start a family. How does that grab you?"

"That sounds like the best idea yet."

Then he said, "And you'll stay home and take care of our house. I'm going to build us a big house in the woods, near a lake. I'll even build you that sundeck you've always wanted."

"Oh Buck," I said. I was so happy.

We spent three lovely gorgeous days where Paulette's name never came up, not one time, and where I only worried a little bit about coming up with the money to pay off the six nights at the Waikiki. I didn't expect God to send me down four or five hundred dollars, but I didn't think he'd let that Visa card go through either. My guess is that He'd figure out a proper way to teach me a lesson, but not a way that would mess up the good thing that me and Buck had going now.

On the fourth morning with Buck, the phone rang. It was Sparkle. She said, "Dixie?"

I said, "What in the hell do you want?"

"I just needed to talk to you. I've been thinking about it, and I just wanted to apologize for leaving you like that."

So I said, "Apologize then." I reached over and rubbed Buck's back. It was smooth, not ripply like when he just finished weight lifting. He reached over and patted my hand and went back to sleep.

Then Sparkle said, "Dixie, I know I owe you the biggest apology. I didn't mean to leave you. It's just that I got so scared thinking of all that money you owed and then I didn't know how to help you get it back and when you blamed me for such an awful thing as telling Renee, well, I just choked up."

"Come on," I said. "Surely you're not going to have me believe you didn't tell her."

"I didn't, Dixie, I swear! I would never do anything like that to you. Please believe me."

With Buck by my side, I was ready to believe anything. So I said, "Oh Sparkle, it's okay. When are you going to realize that nothing is going to come between our friendship. We're bound to have a few ups and downs."

"Dixie, I love you. Listen, you didn't mind me getting together with Donnie, did you? He was really worried we'd hurt your feelings."

I said, "No way. You two are my best friends. Maybe we can get together and have a double wedding ceremony."

Sparkle got real quiet. Then she said, "Oh. Are you back with Buck?"

"Yeah. He's right here beside me, sleeping. And guess what, Sparkle. We've decided to go on ahead and get married this week."

She was quiet again. Then she said, "Does he know about his momma's credit card? What are you going to do about that?"

And so I kind of turned away from Buck and said overly cheerful, "That one I haven't quite figured out yet. Something will come up though, I'm sure. It just has to. And Sparkle, guess what?"

"What?"

"Charlie hasn't come."

"What?"

"You know. Charlie."

"You're pregnant?"

"Yep. And I'm not sure who. Understand?"

Then Sparkle said, "Uh-oh. You're in trouble Dixie!"

"I thought so, too, for a while. But you know what. It just feels like everything is going to be okay now."

Sparkle said, "I see. Well, if this is what you want, Dixie, how about I be your maid of honor?"

"Okay, but I get to pick out the dress. I think I'm going to put you in a nice dull brown." We laughed. Then we hung up. Then I woke up Buck and he and I made love and he didn't even make me pray afterwards.

I fed Buck a healthy room service meal, a manly portion of eggs, grits and sausage patties. Then I shampooed his hair in the Waikiki Jacuzzi and sent him on his way. I had to hit the streets. I had to find a quick way to come up with a quick five hundred dollars and then some. I didn't have to worry about paying off modeling school anymore, but I sure had to worry about that Visa card slipping through the Waikiki computer and processing itself right into Momma Speed's hands. I could just see her now, standing in front of her refrigerator holding that bill, looking confused. And wouldn't Daddy Speed come find me and mow me down then? Wouldn't he just put down his screwdriver and sandpaper wedge and whip my butt!

There's no such thing as a get-rich-quick scheme in Myrtle Beach, South Carolina. You're either already rich driving your Lincoln Continental into town or you're going to stay poor. There just aren't any two ways about it. The only exception was my hero, Vanna White. But she wasn't here and I wasn't her and the only other option I could take was to find Reno and cut a deal with him. Those were the cards I'd been dealt.

Reno, of course, had driven his Lincoln Continental right up to the front door of the Tiger Alley Saloon and made himself a little home there. Girls, girls, girls surrounded him, and GIRLS, GIRLS, GIRLS was what he wanted me to join. It was a strip joint that belonged to a friend of his. I said no to that. He said it wouldn't be so bad. After I got used to it, of course.

What was this thing with men and pornography? It just fascinated me watching them being fascinated by it. It looked to me like you could find a lot more interesting stuff going on in the world than a bunch of naked dancing women.

I said, "Reno. Just forget it. There's no way."

So he said, "Well how about mud wrestling? You can wear a bathing suit doing mud wrestling."

I rolled my eyes. "Got anything else?"

Then he suggested I attend a swinging singles club with him and Jerry. I said no to that, too. So he said there was a new thing he could probably connect me up with, he'd have to make a few calls, called Nintendo Women. I didn't even know what that was, did not even want to venture to guess. "No," I said, "no, no, no, no, NO!" And then I tacked on, "Hey Reno, got any real modeling jobs I can do? You know, the kind where I get to wear clothes and everything?"

That's when old Reno took me aside and said, "Dixie Riggs, let me tell you something. Just between you and me, okay?"

I nodded my head.

He put his arm around me and started walking me around the dance floor. It was too early for the crazy disco lights or the laser show. It was too early for the big afternoon crowd. He said, "Honey, no woman your size is ever going to make it as a high-fashion model. You understand that? I want you to understand that. Now I don't care what they tell you girls at that crazy modeling school, but it takes a full-grown goddess to get on the pages of *Vogue.* Someone like Sparkle. Hell, it's too bad. If you could just get her height or she could just have your face you gals would be in business."

"Reno," I interrupted.

"Just listen. Let me finish. I'm only telling you this because I like you. You've got a future in something, honey, but modeling ain't it."

"Reno, I told you once. I'm not taking my clothes off."

"Okay, okay, I get the picture." We stopped walking and

he took my hands in his. "Well listen kid, I do know this one guy who knows a guy who works at one of the department stores in town. And they're doing some kind of fashion show soon. If you really want me to, I'll see about getting you hooked up."

I threw my arms around him. "Oh Reno! Thank you!"

"But wait," he said, hugging me back. "This isn't going to take care of your money problems. It doesn't pay a red cent."

"Who cares!" I said. Then I added, "Of course, you could always consider lending a good looking gal like me some money."

He grinned and slid his hands down my back and kept on sliding them down. "Oh sweetie. What the boys will be missing tonight. Maybe you'd like to reconsider my first offer."

I hitched his arms back up where they belonged. "Reno, darling, not on your life."

It doesn't make sense that I'm always trying to make sense out of Sparkle when she doesn't make any sense at all. Buck was standing before me, holding out the Waikiki hotel bill. It came to $873. Lordy! Lordy! And he wasn't saying a word. He was just standing there.

I walked past him and made a face of horror to myself. Something told me I wasn't going to be able to think fast enough. I could tell Buck hadn't moved. I could tell that his kind, sweet eyes were following me around the room. He was waiting quietly, quietly waiting for me to tell him it had all been an awful mistake, a mistake awful enough to release him from all the pain that had soaked into his sweet, kind eyes.

I sat down on the deluxe king-size bed and didn't say a word. What could I have said?

"Dixie, Sparkle told me all about it. She was at my house this morning, crying. She's very worried about you. She said you were pregnant. That it was Donnie's baby. That you'd run up Momma's credit card. Do you have anything to say?"

I didn't say anything. If I could have just reached out in front of me and grabbed all my thoughts, pushed them together like I was pushing in an accordion, I might have been able to come up with something. But everything was swirling around my head like the dirt over Pigpen's head in the Charlie Brown comic strip.

"Would you like to clear any of this up for me?" He still stood where he'd been when I'd first come into the room, only he had neatly folded the hotel bill and stuck it into his shirt pocket.

I looked at my shoes.

"Okay, then," he said. "I guess that's it. You've lied so much, I probably wouldn't have believed you if you did say something."

I still didn't say anything.

"Well, just so you know, I loved you, Dixie Riggs. You know that. I really loved you, girl."

I looked up at him. I stared deep into those beautiful green eyes. The end was all there. There would be no more daydreaming of me and Buck together. He had given up. I threw out my last hope. "Buck, for all the information you got, you got some of it wrong," I said. "This isn't necessarily Donnie's baby. As a matter of fact, I'm pretty sure it's yours."

Oh, there is no fear worse than the fear you get when you face an angry man standing in silence.

And there is no greater loss than when he walks out that door without saying a word.

I got in my car and gunned it down the Ocean Boulevard. I didn't even bother to put oil in. I just flew down the road at a hot eighty-five miles an hour to the Pirate Campground Residential Trailer Park. I turned in, passing all the nice double-wides with red and white geraniums planted in window boxes. I passed all the single trailers with chicken-wire fences closing in dirty yards full of dirty toys. By the time I pulled into Donnie's gravel front yard, my car was sounding like rusty rotating helicopter blades. It hurt my ears it was so loud. A car just has to have oil. But I couldn't worry about that now. I parked where Donnie's hot dog mobile would be parked if he was at home, knocked on the door, and beat the shit out of Sparkle Starling. Again.

I said, "You bitch. You whore. You bitch. There's more where that came from," and I beat her up some more. I knocked her into the bedroom and then knocked her back out to the kitchen. I threw her against one wall, and then the other, and I gave her two black eyes and a bloody nose. A pregnant woman can do a lot of damage to someone trying to wreck her home.

I screamed, "Why?"

Sparkle cried, "Wait Dixie. Wait."

"Oh fuck you. I don't want to hear it." Then I beat her up

some more. I probably would have killed her if Donnie hadn't come in and pried me off her.

He said, "Dixie, Dixie. Stop. Look what you've done. You okay, Sparkle? Dixie, you'd better get out of here."

"Oh fuck off," I said. "She looks better that way."

Sparkle cried, "Dixie, let me explain."

"Sparkle, I don't ever want to see you again for as long as I live. If you even come near me, I'll break your fucking nose."

☆

A great sleepiness came over me. I didn't have a move left. I was tired, so tired. All I could focus on was the white line in the road ahead of me. I didn't know where to go. But I needed to go somewhere, badly. I needed to curl up in a corner of a room underneath a black raincoat and melt away until there wouldn't be any more Dixie Riggs left. Until I disappeared. Donnie's was out. Buck's was out. Sparkle's was out of the question, but maybe her mother would take me in. Hell no! But what about my mother? No! No! There was nowhere to go. I was falling apart. I had to get to a hospital. Yes, there was hope at a hospital. Jesus, it was my only hope. I was like a jigsaw puzzle but the colors were wrong, the shapes were wrong. I'd heard of doctors that could make all the pieces fit perfectly instead of trying to jam them into places where they didn't belong, the way I was doing. I would just walk up to the nurse at the front desk and say, "Fix me up please." And she'd whisk me off into a white room where her and the other nurses and an important looking man in a big mustache with a giant clipboard would gather around me and work on me until I turned into a pretty New England 500-piece jigsaw landscape with a covered bridge and blue sky and waving red and gold trees.

But when I got to the front desk of the emergency room at the Myrtle Beach Hospital and told them I needed to check into the crazy ward, QUICK, the orderly raised his eyebrow and asked me about insurance. Well I did not know anything about this insurance stuff. All I wanted was a fast room and a good doctor to push some life back in me, I told him. So he told me to wait in the lobby until I was called.

I watched "The Price Is Right" and drank some coffee, feeling very good about the decision I'd made. Then I drank some more coffee and watched "As the World Turns," and it upset me so much because there was a woman on there who had just discovered she was pregnant and her boyfriend was swinging her around with happiness. So I quit watching that and watched my watch instead and drank more coffee. Then I read a magazine called *Highlights for Children* and tried to find the monkey's hidden bananas on the back page. The coffee was making me a nervous wreck. I'd already peed once and I needed to pee again, but the orderly kept looking at me and I didn't want him to know I was the type that had to go to the bathroom, ever. And okay, this didn't make any sense, but I didn't have to make any sense anymore, because, after all, that's what I was checking in for, wasn't it? I was out of sense.

It seemed like hours went by before a man with a white lab jacket thrown over a loud print Hawaiian shirt came up to me and introduced himself as Dr. Wicker. He leaned down and looked at me through glasses that made his eyes look twice as large as they really were. He reminded me of Mr. Toad in *The Wind in the Willows.* He closed in on me with his bad breath and asked me why I wanted to come to the hospital.

I said, "Because I'm not very happy right now."

He repeated back to me, "You're not very happy right now," as if it was a fact, not a question. Then he bent over and looked at his shoes and began picking the rubber crepe off the sole of the toe points without saying a word. I could see he had a bald spot on top of his head. He could fix that right up with a hat, I thought.

Finally he said, "Well, can you explain that? This unhappiness?"

And so I said, "No. How can you explain unhappiness? I'm just real tired. And I don't know what to do. Can I get a room now?"

He just kept picking at his shoes. He didn't say a word. There was no way in hell I was going to tell this creep about my problems. Finally he said, "Well, ordinarily our procedures are that I check you out first to make sure this is what you really need."

So I said, "Well listen here, buster. It isn't like I come here every day. This is my first time and I mean business. You either take me in there or I'm going to drive my car off the fucking Myrtle Beach pier and I don't care who gives a damn."

The doctor quit picking at his shoes and looked up at me with those magnified eyes and said, "Okay. It's going to take about thirty minutes to get a room ready for you and if you're still interested then, I'll sign you in. Go ahead and fill this out." He gave me a medical history report form and walked away, his shoes sticking to the floor, making a sucking noise as he went down the hospital corridor.

"As the World Turns" turned into "Days of Our Lives" and a half hour turned into a full hour and a half, and another pregnant woman discovered bliss with her lover on TV. I became even more sure that I was doing the right thing. I checked off no on everything about my medical history. No, to high blood pressure. No, to low blood pressure. No, to heart disease, thyroid dysfunction, diabetes. No, to any history of physical illness in my family. How was I supposed to know if Laymen Riggs, the Muff Man, ever got sick? He didn't look sick in his picture and that was all I had to go on. And the only telltale sign of illness on my momma's side of the family was craziness. Grandmother Maybelle was completely off her rocker and as far as I could tell, LeDaire, with her strange ways, had never been exactly right either. Yes indeed, if there had been a box to check off that said mental illness, I'd have put down five stars and circled it three times.

Even when the orderly came down the hall with a wheelchair and made me ride in it to the elevator and up to the fifth floor, I knew I had made the right choice in coming. And I didn't even flinch when they took away my hairdryer, curling iron and shampoo bottle. A crazy didn't need to be worried about curling her hair or straightening it out.

She just needed to worry about getting her head straightened up.

It was only after they put me in a thin white robe with a blue dot print and walked me into a room full of women wearing the same ugly thing that I began to get nervous. One woman sat at a table making paper earrings. She was using the same safety scissors that schoolchildren use. And instead of using Elmer's Glue-All to attach the rhinestones to the earrings, she had a jar of paste by her side, the kind I used to eat in kindergarten.

A real crazy with gray hair and a ratty ponytail kept coming up and playing with my long hair. She wouldn't stop touching it. I said, "If you don't quit, I'll punch you in the mouth."

She said something that sounded like, "Lak dell mesh mon," and laughed. It depressed me so much I walked back to my room and sat on the bed, but some redheaded girl who was a lot more pregnant than me, and with bad teeth, said, "You'll get points taken out of your free time if they catch you on the bed before lights out."

"So. I could care less."

She said, "You won't get to go home when your weekend comes up."

"Shut up and leave me alone."

She said, "I sat on my bed for the first week when I came here and they took away all my privileges. I couldn't even smoke."

And so, not one to smoke, but desperate for something to do, I said, "Do you have a cigarette?"

She said, "You have to buy your own."

I looked around our sad room with the horrible dulled-out orange flowers on the wallpaper pattern and said, "Well look here. If you give me a cigarette, I'll give you a whole pack next time I get one."

She smiled. "Two packs and it's yours." And I wondered why she was here. She was such a smart dealer. She picked up her mattress and pulled out a carton of Kools and a bottle of cough syrup and began to drink the entire bottle. When she was finished she handed me one of the cigarette packs. "Here. Here's them cigarettes. You can have the whole pack, but you'll have to light up in the lobby. Come on, I'll show you where."

We got up and padded down the hall, her in her permanent pink fuzzy bedroom slippers, me in my paper hospital ones, and stood in a line in the recreation room. One by one a girl would go up to a little device built right in the wall—it looked like a doorbell buzzer with a hot ember inside it—and light up her cigarette. And that's what did me in. It wasn't the kindergarten paste. It wasn't the locks on the door. It wasn't the pay phone that was off limits until five. It wasn't even the nurse with the big bosoms and strong perfume. No, it was that awful cigarette lighter. That's when I said, "No more of this. I can't take this. Craziness just isn't for me." And it took that weirdo Dr. Wicker two hours to get back to me and get me out of that place. Two hours of that gray-haired woman playing with my hair and the redheaded girl saying, "Hey, if you leave, when am I going to get my cigarettes back?"

I was at the bottom of rock bottom. I had lost Buck. Buck was gone forever. I'd lost Buck's family. I'd lost my best friend, Sparkle, and I didn't even know why. For the life of me I did not know why she had turned on me. I'd lost my shot at a modeling career. I'd lost everything, everything, everything and I was pregnant. There wasn't even a place for me to stay except the crazy hospital, and I couldn't stay there because it drove me crazy.

It's times like these when you're afraid if you call on God for help, He won't show up. And where would you be then? So you call on your mother instead.

My car was on its last legs, screaming down the road making everyone look at me, making everyone feel sorry for me and be just damned glad it wasn't their car making all the racket. I didn't have enough money for oil. I wouldn't be able to make it to her house without it. And as my luck ran, I didn't even know her number. I hadn't even bothered to find out. So I called the number Johnny D. had slipped me when she hadn't been looking and said, "Johnny D., this is Dixie Riggs. I'm trying to locate my mother."

Johnny D. said, "Oh, hi there, babe. Want to come over? I've got her number around here somewhere. Why don't you come on over while I look for it?"

I said, "No. Just give me her fucking number, would you?"

"Okay, okay. Hold your horses. You know, your mother's a lot nicer than you are."

"Is that so?" I asked.

He laughed. "You bet ya. Here it is."

He gave it to me, I called, and she was at the Wing's pay phone where I was calling from in minutes flat.

☆

One thing about mothers, you don't have to like them for them to like you. I was crying and she said, "Baby doll, just grab your essentials and leave your car in the parking lot. I talked to the manager and he said he wouldn't tow it away. Hop in." She was holding the door of her car open for me.

I couldn't believe I'd called her.

"Come on. Get in. It's going to be all right," she said, as I got in and shut the door. "He, the manager, promised me he'd see what he could do about getting that old car of yours running again. All it took was a little wink here and there and the job's as good as done."

She was so proud of herself. I wanted to throw up.

Momma looked at the picture of Paulette and the box of letters that I'd brought with me and raised her eyebrow. But she didn't say a word. I knew she wanted to ask, but she didn't, and I hated watching her try so hard with me.

She didn't ask me anything. Not why I'd called. Not why I'd been crying. Not where was Buck. I wanted her to so I could bite her head off. I'd have liked to have screamed at her while we drove down the road the same way my car had screamed at me. But she didn't ask a thing. And when she finally did talk, she was pulling into the grocery store. "You sit here a minute. I'm going to run in and get us some grapes," she said.

I didn't watch her get out. I couldn't take seeing her sashaying her little butt across the parking lot. I stared at the smiling pig on the Piggly Wiggly sign instead and wondered what smarty-pants decided to give him a butcher's hat. It was cocked at an angle, the way Paulette's hat was cocked in her picture. I held the picture up and compared it to the pig on the sign. If I squinted out my right eye and completely shut my left one, I could blur her into the pig. It was kind of like superimposing and it made me feel a little better.

I no longer cared about Paulette's relationship with my man, because my relationship with him was over now. What I wanted to know were the small things, like what states she was flying over now; or if she was hanging out at an international airport eating eggs Benedict with a handsome pilot; or writing Buck another letter, trying to screw things up between him and me one last time, which she could no longer do, of course, since things were already as bad as they could be. This time I didn't want to go forward, I wanted to go backward. I wanted to begin at the last letter she'd sent. I wanted to find out how it had ended with them. I whipped off the lavender ribbon and opened the box.

Once again her perfume filled the air.

According to her, Buck had a new dream. He wanted to forget bodybuilding entirely and go straight into acting or modeling, either one. Lord, this was news to me! And there I had been, making him little bodybuilding schedules like an old fool. I should have known. All the signs were there. The way he didn't work out but about thirty minutes a day anymore.

Her response to his dream was to go for it! with a smiley face dotting the *i*. She signed the letter with love and added a P.S. that put a choke hold around my throat. "*P.S. I'll be there next week, Honey-Bean. How about us getting together?*"

LeDaire sashayed up to the car, breaking my concentration. "Oooo, honey, it's hot in here! Turn on that old air conditioner."

"Mom!" I screamed.

"What?" She slammed the door and tossed the paper grocery bag into the backseat and, ignoring my anger, said, "Dixie, make sure you start asking for paper bags. Those plastic ones are killing our wildlife." Then she turned the air conditioner on a whooshing high and, fanning her chest with the receipt, she said, "The price of grapes is skyrocketing!"

She always said it. She always said that grape thing. It

made my neck hairs stand on end. I don't know why it's always such little things that make a daughter hate her mother so. It took absolutely everything for me not to get up in her face and scream, "Shut up, shut up, shut up you redneck, you!"

But she was clueless to the misery she caused me, and clueless to my fear of Paulette's visit. Surely everything was over between me and Buck, but still, still I didn't want her coming down, and still, LeDaire should have seen my pain. But no, not LeDaire. She just smiled with those hot pink lip-glossed lips of hers looking like pure-T white trash, and started up the car.

At her house the evidence was all there. Momma was a redneck, a redneck of the highest order. On the mantelpiece, above a fake log fireplace, were five dishes flanked with tourist scenes on them: Las Vegas, Nevada. Stone Mountain, Georgia. Niagara Falls. How the West Was Won, Wyoming Theme Park. Florida Everglades. She was only thirty-nine years old and already she had one of those fake wood-paneled TV-stereo consoles that old men sit and watch all day long in their easy chairs. The two-toned black-and-burnt-orange wall-to-wall shag rug was in LeDaire's own bad taste, but it was expensive. And the almond-colored kitchen appliances, including a Maytag deluxe dishwasher with economy, normal, and heavy pots and pans setting, was pure evidence that Earl-Dad and Lou were still sending Momma checks. She couldn't have afforded Donnie's Airstream with what was in her bank account. LeDaire would take money from a stranger if he gave it to her. And the funny thing about LeDaire was, strange men were always giving her money. She didn't have to ask. She didn't have to do anything for it. They'd just strike up a conversation with her over a beer or two, see something in those eyes that I obviously had not inherited from her, and pull out their wallets. I wished I had been that lucky.

I laid down on the bubbled plastic that covered her new spring-green couch and pulled a prickly brown afghan over my head and groaned. She said, "Take it easy, kid. Nothing's that bad. And believe me, I've seen bad. If your momma can get out of the fixes she's been in, she can get you out of yours."

"Momma, what are you doing for a living now?"

"Well, it just so happens that Trina Starling has got me a job selling Midnight Madness."

I poked my head out from under the afghan. "The lingerie stuff?"

"Yes. I'll make a lot of money. And Trina'll make money off of me. You see, if you sell this stuff and get someone else to sell it, you make money off of them. Like, I think Trina gets a flat hundred just for getting me started. I'm really going to love this job." She pulled out her new lingerie suitcase. "As a matter of fact," she said, "I'm throwing my very first party this week. I want to get my own career going for a change. For once I want to stop depending on all these men. You know, start a business of my own. I could use your help if you're up to it."

I groaned, "Ohhhh, Momma, I need to sleep."

"Okay, honey," and she let me sleep. She was good about that. She was always good about leaving me alone.

I tossed and turned on the couch, through the late afternoon and into the evening. Every so often I'd wake up sweating, and have to unstick my face from the plastic cover and rub at the imprints on my skin. I was never aware what time it was. Sometimes it seemed like the next day and sometimes it still seemed like night, and it always seemed like hell. My dreams had arms and big thick hands that groped around my soul, choking me with terrible images, mostly of Momma. Every once in a while she'd come over and put a cool compress on my forehead. And whenever I opened my eyes, she'd be stationed in the chair opposite me. It was strange. I could never quite tell where the dreams stopped and she began.

The subconscious is so weird. The people it has me having sex with is so weird. The first dream was about me and Renee and Momma doing sex stuff. Now, I know I'm no lesbian, but still, this disturbed me. I woke up, turned over and had a second dream. This time it was about LeDaire and Daddy Speed. They were married. It was a dream that didn't last too long. Johnny D., the drummer, was their child, but he was also me. And Paulette was baby-sitting me, wearing her Pan American uniform. I sat in a high chair while she showed me the nudie photos of myself.

I flipped over again and went into another dream about Momma and Trina and me trying to hide from Sparkle, who was a general from the Australian 27th war regiment, trying to capture us. We were hiding out in an attic and I was suffocating because they were spraying and styling their hair, not at all concerned about the danger that lay ahead. I had to wake up and pull the afghan off from around my neck where it was wrapped around like a snake, choking me.

And then there was the dream that slapped me in the face with the cold hard facts of my life. It was so close to the truth, I sat straight up on the couch and said, "Yeah, Momma. I'll help you with your lingerie party."

In the dream a man had come looking for me to be his wife. We were so happy together. But the problem was, I expected him to take one look at Momma and flee. Who would want a redneck for a mother-in-law? I had to ask myself. I'd conjure up beautiful pictures of this David or Mike or Steven dream date decked out in a pin-striped suit, and suddenly, out of the blue, and as if I couldn't help it, Laymen, the Muff Man, and Earl-Dad and Lou—Momma's men—would come flying at me like bats out of hell. They'd be saying such things as, "How's my little sapsucker doing?" and mussing up my hair while they said it. And David or Mike or Steven would see this and I would shrink, fade away like the fog they walked off in as they said, "Dixie Riggs, I could have married you if you had come from a decent family. But no decent man would stick around for something like this."

So it came to me in the night, just like in the dream, that I was going to have to change LeDaire. That if it hadn't been for LeDaire, if she had just straightened up and not been so much of a redneck, then I could have straightened up too. I blamed all my problems entirely on Momma. Even though

I'd taken every precaution, precaution after precaution, to keep her white trashiness from rubbing off on me, some of it had just got on and slipped through anyway. It was just unfortunate for me that it had to slip through during my fertile period.

I knew my pregnancy was her fault. It was obvious my sluttiness came from her. I had never worn my hair in layers like she had. And not, under any circumstances, had I ever worn any of the clothes she had bought me. She used to look at me and curl up her lip and say, "Dixie, why on earth do you have on that ugly dress again? I just bought you a nice one."

I'd say, "Momma, I like what I have on."

And she'd say, "Well I don't. You look like something the cat drug in. Go on and change."

But I never would. It was the only battle I had ever won with her while I was growing up. I'd wear my nice clothes and she'd wear her tacky ones, and eventually she'd wear the tacky ones she had bought for me. But then, after all was said and done, it would all end up rubbing off on me anyway. You can't escape the gene pool. So, you see, there wasn't anyone to blame my troubles on but her. She was solely and entirely the one at fault. But I was going to have to be the one responsible enough to find a way out of my hell trap. I was going to have to change LeDaire. I was going to have to find her a good man.

☆

Now changing your mother may sound hard. For the normal person it would be very hard, maybe impossible. However, I have a genius mind. I have what you call street smarts. I'm not sure how to describe that exactly, except to say that I can put two and two together and come up with the whole story on what makes someone tick. Everyone that is except Buck, and maybe Sparkle.

I could have kicked myself for not having thought of it sooner, the plan, I mean. If I had worked on LeDaire when I was at, say, age thirteen or fourteen, we would probably still be sitting at the Speeds' dinner table now, laughing up a storm. And every time Momma Speed would get up from the table to get more tea, corn bread or butter, she'd pat my stomach and say, "I can't wait for you to marry my son and have yourself a little Buck."

Oh, how I missed my Buck.

A woman can make a lot of mistakes when she misses a man so bad she can't swallow. For instance, showing up at his house unexpected is one of them.

I pulled LeDaire's car into Buck's driveway and parked it next to the pickup truck he'd been painting forever. I knocked on the door and no one answered so, like always, I just walked on into the house unannounced. That's when I saw Sparkle. She was on the floor of Buck's bedroom dry-shaving her legs with only her panties on.

I said, "What are you doing here?"

Sparkle jumped. "Oh Dixie! You scared me for a minute there. How are you?" she asked, running over to me like I needed a wheelchair.

"Get your hands off me. What's going on here?" I asked again.

"Well," she said, sitting on Buck's bed, making herself at home. "I came by a couple of days ago, God, or was it yesterday? Boy, I can't remember. So much has happened." She fell back on Buck's pillows. "Anyway, I was worried sick about you and I didn't know who to come to. So I came to Buck and, well, you really hurt him, Dix. You really did."

"Sparkle, get to the point."

She looked at me confused and sat back up. "You mean, me being here and all?"

I gave her the silent treatment. Like I've said before, it is always a good thing to store up your energy before you beat the shit out of somebody.

"Well, I don't know what to say. One thing led to another. Buck needed a friend and I needed a place to stay. I'm sorry."

"You're sorry."

"Yeah, I'm sorry. I just said so." Sparkle started to get defensive. "And don't think about beating me up again, because Buck's in the garage painting my car right now, and he'll hear me scream if you do."

"Buck's painting your car," I said flatly. "Well, that's nice. That's just real nice of him."

Sparkle softened up. "Dixie, don't get upset now. A girl in your condition should try and stay calm," but I was already out the door.

I should have known. Lord, God, can a woman be so dumb. It was right there in front of my face the whole time. Sparkle's words were whirling around inside me: "I hate Buck." "What a creep." "I can't stand him." "Why don't you get rid of him and get a real man." "You should have left him a long time ago." It was a classic case of the fine line between love and hate. She hated him so much she loved him. Or maybe it had been all love right from the beginning.

Like I said, sometimes there's only one thing a girl can do when she gets red hot, and that's to visit Donnie Sessions. Only I wasn't red hot horny this time, I was red hot angry.

After my car, LeDaire's car was a pleasure to drive. One, because I didn't have to fill it up with oil. Two, because it had a 160-horsepower V-8 engine that could burn rubber when you left or arrived anywhere mad.

Donnie was just getting into his hot dog mobile when I screeched up. He said, "Whoa! Slow down, Momma. What's up?"

I said, "Can we talk?"

"Yep. Want to go for a ride? Got to deliver some dogs."

So I said, "Sure," and we drove off down the road, turning right onto the Ocean Boulevard.

The wind blew through my hair and it pulled the dress I was wearing tight across my stomach. I was getting a little tummy. It wasn't big enough to be a pregnant tummy, but it was something. I was becoming a mommy whether I liked it or not.

Donnie drove with one arm resting on the steering column and the other arm hanging out the side of the car. He kept staring at me. "Want to tell me what's up?" he asked.

"Donnie, tell me about you and Sparkle. When did yall break up?"

"Break up? We were never together."

I said, "But what about you picking her up at the hotel? She said yall were going to live together. That yall were in love."

"She told you that? Hell, she told me you kicked her out."

"What?" That's when I explained the whole picture to him, from the beginning to end. I told him the whole porno story, the story about Renee kicking me out of school and the story of how all that led up to Sparkle living with Buck. Except for the pregnancy thing, I talked like I'd never talked before.

Donnie just listened as he drove past Pirate Putt-Putt, Mammy's House of Pancakes and on past the old Pavilion to a hot dog stand on the side of the road.

Finally I wound down and he stopped the car. "Shit."

"I know," I said.

"She oughtn't to have treated you like that, girl."

"I know. The hard thing is, I would have done anything for her. Did I ever tell you how we met?"

He grinned at me. "Nope."

"We were at the beach trying to pick up the same lifeguard. But he turned out to be such a creep, we both walked off together and left him sitting at his station not knowing what happened. Up until yesterday, we hadn't spent a day apart."

Donnie reached over and kissed me on the forehead. "Wait here. I got to get this man his foot-longs before he blows a gasket."

So I sat and waited. It was hot and the salty ocean air made my skin sticky and my hair frizzy. I fiddled with Donnie's rearview mirror and made faces at myself. I looked so ugly. I wondered if LeDaire had felt this ugly when she was pregnant with me. I curled my lip and turned the mirror away and tried to think about something besides Sparkle and Buck. My man in love with my best friend. Oh, it was the worst of all things.

Donnie jumped back into the hot dog mobile and picked up where he'd left off. "You know, for being such a rotten little girl, I kind of liked that kid. I wouldn't have minded going out with her."

"I can see that," I said. "She's a pretty girl."

"You know, you ain't going to like this," said Donnie, "but I figure I'd better be the one to tell you."

I pressed my stomach. A sick feeling came over me. "Shoot."

"Okay," he said. He took a deep breath. "Buck's joined up at that modeling school."

"Oh my God."

"But Dixie, I don't think it took a lot of talking to get him to go, is what I'm saying. That's one man who's hung up on his looks, if you know what I mean."

"I can't believe this, Donnie."

"Well, girl, that's not all. From what she told me, Sparkle quit that big class she was in so she and Buck could take private lessons together. They're supposed to go down there every afternoon and learn to work with each other as a couple or something. Sounds creepy to me."

I crumpled on the seat. I covered my face with my hands and started crying. "It's like I've handed him over to that little bitch on a silver platter."

"There, there," he said, patting my leg.

"Donnie, you think I'm pretty, don't you?" I asked, wiping my eyes.

He grabbed me and hugged me. "Pretty, you're a real looker, darling."

"Well Donnie, would you ever marry me?"

He pulled away immediately, stiffening up on his seat. "Why?" he asked, faking a yawn.

"I don't know. It's just that I was kind of wondering if I'd be the sort of woman a man would like to marry?"

He yawned again. "Well, yeah. I guess there'd be a man out there for you."

I smoothed my dress over my pregnant stomach. "But you don't think you'll ever get married?" I asked.

"Um, no. I don't think so."

"It's okay, Donnie. I wasn't proposing. I just wanted to

know." I started crying again. God almighty, even the bottom of the barrel, the last choice on earth did not want to marry me. I wailed.

Donnie was frantic. "Hold up, doll baby. Hold up. It just come to me. I know what we can do."

"Yeah?"

"Well, I just think I might have a little plan to get you back on the road and show that Sparkle a thing or two in the process. You interested?"

I was interested all right. Who would have ever thought Donnie Sessions had so many brains? He'd sure thrown me for a loop.

He took me to the beauty parlor and paid for me to get my hair cut and styled. Well, actually what he paid for was for me to get my hair done, which meant washed. For as you know, men do not like for a woman to cut her long hair. But there were two golden rules out there in love land if you found you'd lost your man's love. The first one was, never show your lover a picture of any of the goofy guys that might be courting you on the side. Because honey, they may look goofy to you, but as long as he doesn't know that, and as long as they keep calling you up, they are competition in his mind. If his love starts slipping, you say, "Yoo-hoo, so and so called today," and it works every time. The second rule is, if that doesn't work and all else fails, get a new look. It is always exciting to a man to think he has a new woman on his hands. My figuring on this is that they get the added excitement of messing around with another woman and at the same time they remain monogamous to you. Sure, the average woman might come up to me on the street and say, "Dixie Riggs, there you go again, not making any sense." But I'd just have to answer back and tell her to try it out and then come to me with her complaining. There would be none.

So I told the hairstylist at Fantastic Sam's to bring out my alter ego. And he whipped me around in that chair and chop chop chop, I was getting my long coal black hair cut into a sweet pageboy flip.

While I was doing that, Donnie drove to Wing's where my old car was broke down and got out some of the new clothes that I'd bought on Momma Speed's credit card. Then he took them for a good cleaning and pressing at the Burnett's dry cleaning store, and while he waited, he went over to Sears and bought me a pair of white sandals that were way too big and really gross looking, like something Grandmother Maybelle would have worn. But it was the thought that counted.

"Oh, Donnie. You shouldn't have," I said, holding them out in front of me like meat gone bad.

He stared at me in horror. "Dixie. You cut your hair off."

"You bet. Don't you love it?" I asked, swinging around in a circle.

"Not really," he said, shaking his head.

"Well, you will when I put that dress on."

Thirty minutes later, Donnie and I were standing across from Renee's and he was still trying to feel me off.

"Quit." I laughed.

"Dixie, you never looked so good."

I had on a cute little Betsey Johnson black number that really qualified for underwear. It was tight, with a fishnet backing. The afternoon sun beat hot on my brown summer shoulders and I knew I looked good. Hell, standing there hiding behind an old station wagon waiting for Buck to show up, I could've given Vanna White a run for her money.

"Are you ready?" Donnie asked.

"Yep, but I'm nervous as a dog."

"Good. It's always better to be a little nervous. Whenever I'm nervous, I sell a lot more hot dogs than if I'm feeling real sure of myself." He squeezed my waist and slid his hand on down.

I looked at him. I studied him hard. He just looked so

dumb, but his idea was so smart. It went like this: If what Casey had said was true, about Renee keeping her girls in their skintight contracts if she even thought she smelled success, then he thought we should give it a try. He said she'd jump at the chance to take me back into school, hell, she'd even put me straight into the agency, if we could get her to believe some top people were after me.

We'd brainstormed the whole thing in a matter of minutes. And we'd executed it about as fast. First, we made a call to Reno-Richard. Well, Donnie made it. At the time, I was too weak to believe anything would work. So I had just dialed the number, introduced them over the phone and let them take over. I don't know what all Donnie told him, but whatever it was, it worked, because Reno then made a call to his friend, who made a call to *his* friend, and now I was registered to be a model in the Newberry's Department Store's upcoming fashion show.

And that wasn't all. Reno, bless his sweet heart, had even made up a fake agency contract and given it to Donnie, who went over to the Tiger Alley and picked it up, in between buying the shoes and getting the dry cleaning done.

Well I wasn't weak now. I was strong and feeling stronger. I wasn't sure I could ever get Buck back, but at least I would look damn good not doing it. And I had a big feeling that the contract I was holding in my hand would lead me down Renee's runway again very soon. It was just a matter of waiting it out, then walking into her place and slapping that sucker down on her desk at the right time.

I waited fifteen minutes, then I went on in. It was important for me to capture Buck and Sparkle in the middle of something. And I did. Renee had them pretending they were posing for a catalog. Their movements were choppier than runway modeling, which all kind of flowed together. This was a more precise kind of movement. Buck seemed to know instinctively when something wasn't working. You could tell by the way he'd readjust his hands at the last minute. Lord, he was a natural. They were putting their weight on the back of their feet, except Sparkle looked like maybe all her weight was on Buck. And you know, they looked real good together. I had to give them that. It was breaking my heart.

Renee pushed them this way and that, then she sat down on the runway and studied them both. She pushed at her hair and said, kind of to herself more than them, "Catalog modeling is a very rigorous field, surprisingly competitive. It's not as hard as high-fashion modeling. Now that's hard. I mean, there are so many good looking people out there, it comes down to who you know, or how trendy you look."

She got up and walked around Sparkle, holding her out at arm's length, scanning her body for flaws. Then she did the same to Buck but she was real touchy-feely with him. "Yes, I think we can get you both some good work in catalogs.

Buck, you might be able to make it in the magazines. But Sparkle doesn't have much of a chance with that face. No." She shook her head. "It's too ordinary. It's pretty, but not pretty enough. Well," she sighed. "Enough of that. Let's get back to work. Can yall get just a little closer?"

They moved in closer, trying not to mess up their poses. Most normal couples didn't stand that close, but it was funny how you accepted it as a natural look. It was kind of like in the movies when you see three men all jammed together in the front seat of a car. You don't think anything of it unless you look real close and see they're practically sitting on each other's laps and there's no one sitting in the backseat.

Renee rolled her eyes and clapped. "Okay boys and girls closer! I know it feels unnatural, but the camera will take care of that. Get used to posing practically on top of each other." Sparkle snuggled up closer to Buck, and he leaned in to her, hooking his wrists up in such a way that he looked ready to spring.

"Sparkle," Renee said. "Get that pout off your face. This is not *Playboy.* This is an exercise to teach you how to pose for J. C. Penney type catalogs. Just blow out and smile natural. Okay. Good."

It was funny that Sparkle was such a natural at having her picture taken with no clothes on, but put that little weasel in a dress and she lost all her moves. With enough direction, Renee finally got Sparkle looking the way Buck did, like all their sex had been taken out of them. Their faces looked too pleasant. They looked like mannequins. Like Ken and Barbie.

Renee got behind the video camera and began filming. She was taping them so she could play back their flaws and strengths for them. "Okay," she said. "Buck, I want to see you do a few stances alone. Sparkle, put on another outfit."

There was a box on the floor filled with clothes. Sparkle had giant clips all up and down the back of the outfit she was wearing, big old strong clips and duct tape that made her clothes fit tight, like an instant tailor. When she bent over, the clips started popping off. And she still looked miserable about Renee calling her ordinary.

It was my cue. Walk in like a love goddess while my opponent was down. I put a little of LeDaire's sashaying into my walk and gave a three-quarter French military turn for some added spin at the end. And I said, "Renee, I know we've had our differences here, but I've just got to have some help. I've been offered this contract, and I don't know who else can look it over but you. Oh. Hey Buck. Am I interrupting anything?"

While Renee looked at the contract, I made sure Buck was looking at me. I looked skinny skinny standing there in my little Betsey Johnson. The hard part was making sure I kept my little pregnant tummy sucked in. I couldn't have been more than eight or nine weeks, tops, but I swear I had to be careful. Every once in a while, just for effect, I'd smooth my hands down my waist and sigh.

Renee said, "Well listen, this is no good."

"What do you mean?" I said. "Of course it's good." I didn't even know what it said. I'd tried reading it, but I couldn't follow word one.

"They want too much. And who is this agency anyway? Did you check them out to see if they were reputable? They're trying to rip you off, you know." Renee pulled me down to sit with her, then she went over everything with a fine-tooth comb and said, "So you see. Now, if you want, I can place you in our agency and give you the same kind of deal at a cheaper price."

I scrunched my lips and looked thoughtful. I had to play this one out.

"Look," she continued. "Since you seem to have gotten such a head start by yourself, and you're so pretty, I'll even give you a discount. Want to take a shot at it?"

"Well, I don't know," I said, drawing it out. Then I smiled at her, my brightest smile, full teeth, and I crossed my legs at Buck, my sexiest leg cross to date, and I said, "Hey, okay, it looks like you got yourself a little deal."

Buck stayed where he was and Sparkle came over to me. "Congratulations Dixie."

I smiled brilliantly at her. "Thanks, hon."

"You got your hair cut. It looks great," she said, smiling like a knife.

I swung my hair around freely, like Paulette had done in her picture, hoping Buck was watching. "Yep, I most certainly did. The agency paid for the whole thing," I lied.

She said, "Well that's good. I better get back to my exercises. You ready, Buck?" she called out to him as she walked back to where he stood, an ice prince.

Of course, you can bet I smelled good too. I'd finally figured out Paulette's perfume. It was Opium, and I'd spent the better part of the last hour spraying it up and down my legs, behind my ears and once, even on my bosoms. Oh and did my new pregnant bosoms ever look voluptuous squeezed into my little black Betsey Johnson. And I made a point of walking past Buck on my way out the door. If my new look didn't bring love back to Buck, maybe the fragrance would. If he didn't want to think about me, I'd at least have him thinking about Paulette instead of Sparkle. I could handle Paulette now. Isn't it funny how these things change around?

My job was only half done. I'd gotten my modeling career back on track, but I still had to change Momma into somebody I could offer up as a suitable mother-in-law. It was a slim chance that it might be the ticket to building me and Buck back into a couple. It was slim, but it was the only chance I had, and I had to jump on it.

Donnie had been real helpful in the Renee scheme. And I know it sounds horrible, but after it was all over we drove until we couldn't stand it anymore, parked in the nearest parking lot and made love right there and then in his hot dog mobile. I looked just too damned good not to be made love to.

But what I had to do with Momma, he couldn't help me with. It was just between her and me. So he dropped me off at her house, but not before making love to me again right there in her own front yard. It was dark by then, but still, even Dixie Riggs should know better than that.

LeDaire was sitting in her La-Z-Boy watching the J. C. Penney Home Shopping Channel on TV. She was making a list of all the goodies she was going to buy. "Oh Dixie, look at these cute little figurines," she said to me as I walked in the door. "Wouldn't they look cute on the mantelpiece."

If men could only see LeDaire while she watched TV in

her quilted bathrobe that had been around as long as the Bible. For a minute there she actually looked like a mother. But I had to remember that underneath that quilted robe she was probably wearing a red leather miniskirt and a pair of sizzling stilettos.

I said, "LeDaire, let's work on your party. Let's make some money for you so you can afford all those figurines."

LeDaire was like a child. She brightened up right away. She loved planning parties. We sat on the floor with the TV off and I let her have full range. She could pick the time, the place, the food, the drinks, everything. Everything but the men. That part was up to me.

"I don't think I like that," she said.

"Well you don't have to like it. You just have to make money. And I'm going to find the people who'll do you the most good."

She smirked at me and then she reached over and pretended to zap me with the remote control. "You know, I haven't seen you this happy since the last time you saw Earl-Dad. If it means that much to you, by all means, take over."

I was cooking. I let her plan everything, and then, in my smoothest Dixie Riggs way, I changed all her plans into mine. She didn't even know what hit her until the night of the party.

We had placed an ad in the classified section of the *Myrtle Beach Sun Times.* Not under Miscellaneous or Personal, but smack dab in the middle of Business Employment. LeDaire had said, "But Dixie, that doesn't make any sense."

I had said, "Of course it does, Momma. You see, if we let these men know that there's an opportunity for them to make money *and* meet women *and* on top of that be able to buy their wife or girlfriends some sexy lingerie without having to go into the stores, they'll come in flocks."

"Well," she had said. "You've got a point. Even I can't get a man to enjoy going to the mall. They just buckle under, don't they?" We both cracked up. That was weird. Up until then I don't think we'd ever laughed together.

So we placed the ad, you know, the normal kind of WANTED: MEN WITH A DESIRE TO SELL AND BUY LINGERIE WITHOUT THE EXTRA

BURDEN OF THE MALL SCENE. You wouldn't have liked it; still, we did. And we went home to wait for four nights, for the night of the party.

We got to know each other a little bit, me and Momma, when she was home that is. She had a date out about every night, which was fine with me because it gave me time to pack all her redneck plates and other crap in boxes and store them up in the attic.

You see, my plan was a simple but genius one. I figured most men who read the business section of the classifieds wore suits. A good start to finding a classy man for your mom. And okay, so some of them are married and some have girlfriends, but there had to be a few desirable bachelors in the group. And if it was just a matter of a girlfriend, not a wife, well hell, LeDaire wasn't beyond stealing a sexy man from another woman. All was fair in love and war. I figured if I could just get these men interested in selling Momma's product, then automatically these men would have something in common with her. That's what everyone says a good relationship is based on, things in common.

So when the night of the party was upon us, I was ready. Like I said, we'd had a few nights of preparation. And when LeDaire wasn't out tramping around, she was at home on the phone like a teenager. Meanwhile, I had done a lot of grieving for Buck, a lot of daydreaming about getting him back. And I had cooked. And I had pregnantly eaten, half of just about every hors d'oeuvre I'd cooked.

Buck hadn't called. I hadn't expected him to. But I'd gotten plenty of hang-up calls and I loved every one of those. I'd lean back on the refrigerator and dream they were him calling to hear my voice. Oh yeah, and Renee had called about fifteen times. I think she wanted to keep her hand in the pot. She wanted to remind me of this. She wanted to remind me of that. She wanted to remind me that there was a fashion show for Newberry's in a few days that she wanted me to be in. I told her to sign me up. I wasn't about to tell her I was already signed. I wanted her to find that out on her own and be taken aback. I wanted her to think agents were signing me up all over town, I was such a hot ticket.

Well, anyway, the night of the party was on us and I called Momma to get off the phone QUICK! "We have got to get ready," I said.

"Okay. Which outfit should I wear?"

I said, "This one." I held up a sweet white linen dress suit, courtesy of my Newberry's splurge, and told her to put it on. "I'm sure we wear the same size." I wasn't, really. LeDaire, as I'd said before, had a blocky midwaist. However, I'd taken the trouble to pull out a few seams here and there. I'd just have to cross my fingers.

"I'm not wearing that," she said. She fingered it. "It's a nice dress, but it ain't going to sell shit."

"What?"

"Dixie, I'm supposed to greet these people wearing one of the outfits. That's what the booklet says. How else are they supposed to know what these things look like?"

I paced the room. I sat down on the bed and then got right back up. "You're not thinking about really doing that, are you? I mean, really Momma."

"Yes, I am." She began pulling a micro short pink teddy out of the suitcase. It had wild red appliqués shaped like hands patched onto the breast part.

I grabbed it from her. "You are not wearing anything but this damned suit," I said, throwing it at her.

"Okay, okay," she said. "I'll wear the suit. Just calm down. Go on in there and answer the door, okay. I'll be okay."

Lord! Why did God see fit to give me a momma like LeDaire, my cross to bear in this life! I breathed the biggest sigh of relief there ever was walking out of that room. To think she actually didn't even know any better than to wear something like that.

She called out after me. "Oh, I forgot. Lou's coming too. If you get to him before I do, would you explain the party to him. I forgot to tell him about it."

"Ohhhh, Momma! No! You can't invite him."

And she said, "Well, what'll you have me do? Leave him out in the car then? No, Dixie, he's going to come and that's that."

I cringed to think of it. In one way, Lou was the worst of

all her boyfriends. He always wore disco jeans and black lace-ups. And as if that weren't bad enough, he greased his hair back with Vitalis. Yuk, yuk, yuk, was what I thought. "But Momma, don't you think he'll be out of place sitting next to all those men wearing suits?"

"Well I'm sure Lou has a suit in the car. Don't worry, he'll fit in just fine."

I had to give her a little room, and besides, once she saw the class the other men had, Lou would blend in with the woodwork. He'd be on his way back to Cordele the next morning and LeDaire would be on her way into a nice romance with a stylish man who I could proudly introduce to the Speeds. And this stylish man would see that Daddy Speed and his family might just be a little bit redneck, but he'd know they were the salt of the earth type rednecks, the type you'd want your stepdaughter marrying into. Not the type that slutted their way from town to town like a bunch of Gypsies. Yes, Lou was the only hitch in my parade, but at least there was going to be a parade.

Naturally, Lou was the first to arrive. He looked worse than I remembered and I couldn't even look at him while he talked about his store and the lawyers and how much he missed LeDaire. "Miss away," I thought, as I carried the cakes and pies and bacon-wrapped livers out from the kitchen, "for tomorrow you'll be heading home without her. Yes, indeedy."

"What is this party, anyhow?" asked Lou. "We were supposed to eat at that Japanese steak house tonight. She must've forgotten."

"Yes," I said. "I guess she did. MOMMA!" I yelled. "Are you ready yet?"

"Almost," she yelled back. "I think somebody else just pulled in the driveway. Is Lou here yet?"

I ignored her and smoothed my casual skirt down and left Lou sitting in the kitchen trying to figure it all out.

The first candidate wasn't bad at all. A love god! Future husband material. He said he was in stocks. I checked for a wedding ring or a white line where one could have been and he was clean. He wore a fine pin-striped suit and he didn't use oil in his hair. He wore black socks and he sat down on the couch to wait. And when I offered him scotch, he said he only drank coffee!

Then came the second candidate, the married man, and I told him he must have the wrong house. Hey. I figured if I could spot them, I might as well try and weed them out.

He held out a piece of paper and said, "Well this is 1414 Monroe Street, isn't it?"

And I said, "Give me that." I looked at it hard and said, "This must be a practical joke," and sent him on his way. As he drove off, a banker drove up. Now this man was most certainly single. He had that I-need-a-woman-bad look about him. He was even better looking than the stockbroker. He even wore a vest!

By eight-oh-five, we had seven bachelors in our living room, one token married man who wouldn't go away for nothing, and Lou in his nightmare green leisure suit with the fancy white stitching. Like I said, I do not know much about men's clothes, but I did know that this wasn't the kind of suit I wanted my mother taking to get dry cleaned.

I poked my head down the hallway and yelled, "Momma, they're here. Hurry up!"

While we waited for her, I served the pie and chatted it up with every man but Lou, who just sat on the couch staring straight ahead. I said this or that to this man and that or this to that man and finally I stood up and said to all of them, "Tonight LeDaire Rideout, my mother, is going to introduce you to the world of lingerie. LeDaire are you ready yet?"

"I'm on my way," I heard her say. And I could hardly breathe I was so excited. Everything was coming together so nicely. Renee had taken me back, and soon Momma would walk out and see all those nice men sitting next to Lou and her past would flash through her mind like a bad movie. I could almost see the transformation come over her face when she made her shy entrance into the living room. She would not be able to help comparing the banker in his vest to Lou. She'd smooth down the front of her fine linen suit not feeling like her old self, but feeling the crispness of her new self coming over her. I sat down on the La-Z-Boy. I wanted LeDaire to be the only woman standing when she made her entrance. I believe in that first impression. I held my breath and thought about Buck. I just wished he could be here for this.

"Jesus!" I said it out loud. I couldn't believe it. Momma came walking in in a full circle wearing that horrid little teddy with the red hand appliqués sewn on the bosom! Oh my word! Oh my God! She hadn't! She had! Lou sat up straighter. So did every other man.

"LeDaire!" I said.

"Hey darlings," she said to the men, winking at me. "If you want to put the life back in your love life, have I got some helpers for you." She twirled around. "Tonight, you can just sit back and relax. Maybe buy something for the missus. Maybe you'll be interested in starting a business of your own." She put her hands on her thighs and began rocking back and forth, talking, explaining the pyramid money plan for Midnight Madness Lingerie. It was full energy for LeDaire. She wasn't missing a beat.

I thought for sure the classy men would leave and Lou would stay, but it turned out to be the reverse. They didn't budge and Lou went in the kitchen. Then Momma said, "I'll be right back with another one of Midnight Madness Lingerie's best sellers. Dixie, see if they need another drink."

I followed her out, then I ran back in and told the men to hold on a second, and then I went back to the bedroom where LeDaire was pulling the teddy over her head. "What in the hell are you doing? What in the blessed fuck are you doing?" My voice was rising. I couldn't keep it down. I was shaking.

"Calm down, honey," she said, snapping a push-up bra over her breasts. "Lord, you'd think you were on your period every day of your life."

I couldn't believe I was hearing this. My own mother! "Momma, what happened to the suit? The clean-cut white suit I ironed for you?"

She pulled on a silk waist slip, light blue with a lace hem. "I couldn't put that on, Dixie. Nobody would have bought anything then."

"You can't wear that, Momma. Don't you dare walk out of this room with that on!"

"Maybe you're right," she said, examining herself in the mirror. "I look like an underwear commercial. I need a little more pizzazz, don't I? I'm not used to this stuff yet." She removed the slip and slipped into some French-cut panties instead. "Is this any better? Nah. I'll try a garter belt, too."

"No, Momma. No. That's not what I'm saying." I wiped away my tears. "I got the suit so you'd look like someone with class. You look like a whore now." I couldn't stop crying. My heart was pounding against my rib cage.

"Nonsense. Dixie, this is business. Now just stay in here and take it easy. There's no point in you ruining this party just because you don't have a sense of humor." With that, she left and was out the door and down the hall.

I was mortified. I went through the suitcase and started pulling everything out of it. The plastic bottles of gels with the smiling women on them that read "Hawaiian Nights" and "Piña Colada Madness," the pink bras and blue satin bras, the lace ones, and threw them all to the side. I was frantic to get rid of them. Finally I just grabbed them up and threw them out the windows onto the azalea bushes.

I ran down the hall as fast as I could, into the living room, picked up the brown afghan from behind the men on the couch and I threw it over Momma's shoulders. And then I started screaming. I was crying and shrieking and screaming and crying and yelling for those men to leave. "Get out! Get out! Get out of here NOW!" I sounded like a cat in pain. The room was too hot. The men were too large, the living room was too small, smaller even than the small beady eyes of the men, whose eyes got even smaller, and beadier. And at the same time they got bigger and bigger and bigger and right up on me, and I was back in the room with LeDaire holding on to me before I knew what had happened. She said, "Oh baby, you're breathing too hard. Calm down, calm down. What have I done?"

I shrieked with pain.

"Oh my baby," she said. "Come on, you need some fresh air."

I cried, "Momma? What's wrong with me?"

She walked me to the back door and sat me down on the steps outside. "Shhh, shhh. Oh baby, what have I gone and done?"

I wailed, "But Momma, I'm the one that's done those sleazy contests, and had those awful pictures of me taken. Why did this bother me? I'm the whore. What's wrong with me? I'm so confused."

She said, "Honey, there's not a damn thing wrong with you. Those pictures weren't meant for anybody's eyes but yours, and those contests, well, you needed the money. And there's nothing wrong with that. But this is different. I'm your momma, the only one you'll ever have, and you want me to *be* your momma, not some tramp." She squeezed me so tight I could hardly breathe. "But I'm just one big mistake after another where you're concerned. If I could take it all back, I would. But I love you, Dixie girl. I love you so much." She rocked me back and forth and cried softly in my hair.

"Oh Momma," I cried.

We sat out there on the back steps with the slugs, she with just the garter belt and bra on. I could feel the goose bumps on her arm. It wasn't cold, it was summer, but there was a cool breeze coming in. The yellow bug light turned our faces as orange as the makeup LeDaire had on. She rubbed my head and I wished with all my heart that I wasn't all grown up and out there on my own without Momma there to rub my head all the time. I said, "Momma?"

She said, "Yeah baby? My baby girl," holding me against her, rocking me gently back and forth and back and forth.

"Momma, I'm pregnant."

LeDaire sat there, quiet, just rocking. Then she said, "Oh my poor baby. What can I do for you, Dixie? I'll do anything you want."

I think about this an awful lot. About what LeDaire can do for me. Usually it always comes down to her not being a redneck anymore. But this time I didn't think that. This time I thought of her in a different light. I could back up and see her and Trina, Sparkle's momma, both as younger girls going out and entering those same stupid sleazy contests I had done, trying to figure out what life was all about, and how to make money, how to survive. Suddenly I could see them both, LeDaire and Trina, looking just like me and Sparkle, and I understood. It came to me like a cloud lifting right out of my head. If you're poor, you're probably always going to be making sleazy mistakes. And if you're just lucky enough not to be poor, you're probably going to make the same mistakes but wear better clothes making them. And no matter who you want your momma to be, or who you want to be like, you're never going to change a fucking thing, because life is basically like a bigger version of high school. You either had a good reputation, or you didn't. You either passed your finals, or you didn't. You either got to go off for first week at the beach to a rented beach house, or you got to go and sleep in the car. You either went to the prom and stayed there, or you never went at all and spent the rest of your life figuring out why.

It's like people always go around saying the way to feel better about your enemy is by imagining them in their underwear, well that was all wrong. I figure if you can imagine what someone was like in high school, you'll be ahead of their game. I wasn't sure what this all meant, because I've never been the clearest thinker, but I knew one thing. I knew it meant that the only changing to be done around here had to come from me. I didn't have to change LeDaire, just my way of seeing her. She wasn't bad. Hell, her type was the salt of the earth, just like Daddy and Momma Speed, only she salted the earth with a little more spices.

I said, "Momma, you aren't a redneck."

"What?"

Then Lou came back and opened the screen door and said, "Sadie," because he always calls my momma Sadie. "Sadie, what on earth has happened here? What did you have your mind on, doing a thing like this?"

She said, "Lou, would you mind leaving me and Dixie alone a bit longer?"

He said, "Sadie, I think I'm going to tell those men to go on home now. Yall just take your time." He unbuttoned his jacket and hitched up his pants and I noticed that his white socks were even whiter than Momma's push-up bra. He reached down and rubbed my head and said, "Hey, you little sapsucker. You okay, girl?"

I didn't say anything. He took off his green leisure jacket and wrapped it around Momma and then he left. Then I said, "Hey Momma, remember when we first moved in with Lou? You know, after Earl-Dad?"

She said, "Yeah?"

"Well, didn't you say he wanted to marry you?"

She said, "Yep. But I wasn't ready yet."

"Are you now?"

"Well, sometimes I think I am and sometimes I just think I want to ride this one out for a while, like maybe I want to do something right for a change."

So I said, "Well, at first I couldn't stand him, but for the life of me I can't remember why. Maybe marrying Lou would be a good thing after all."

"Dixie," she said suddenly. She pulled me away from her and looked me hard in the face. "Can you tell me what's going on with you now? The whole story. The one with you and Sparkle. Trina told me some of it. I want to know the rest."

We sat there and listened to the bankers and the stockbrokers revving up and pulling out across the gravel. Then I told her everything, up to and including Sparkle setting me up just about any chance she got. About how much I loved Buck, and how much I owed on Momma Speed's Visa card, and how I was going to die right on the spot if I really had to accept that I'd lost Buck for good, which I had, of course, due to Sparkle, of course, and, well, just everything. For the first time in my life it felt so good not to have to lie. I couldn't believe I hadn't lied about *something.* So I searched my mind one last time and then I told her about how Buck and Donnie, either one, could be the daddy of my baby.

When I was finished she said, "Dixie, don't you worry about anything. You hear me? I've done so little for you. Now's my chance to finally do something good. I'll take care of the whole thing."

"Momma?"

She said, "You don't have to call me Momma this time. This time I'm going to help you out even if you just call me plain old LeDaire."

We both laughed and sat back against the screen door and listened to the last car pull out. Then we heard Lou rattling around in the kitchen. He was washing dishes, putting them away.

Finally she said, "Dixie?"

"Yeah, Momma?"

"What did you say to me a minute ago? That thing you said before Lou came out. What was that all about?"

"Oh. That. I just said you weren't a redneck."

She kind of laughed. "A redneck?"

"Yeah, you're not a redneck after all."

40

Renee would not leave me alone. The next day was the morning of Newberry's fashion show and she was calling every thirty minutes to remind me of something else. It was, "Dixie, don't forget you'll be in the wind so wear a lot of hairspray," and, "Dixie, I forgot to tell you to bring an extra pair of high heels in case something goes wrong," and, "Dixie, don't forget you'll be wearing a bathing suit."

I was totally exasperated with her. "So what? What about a bathing suit?"

"Well, shave, you know. There'll be some talent scouts there who always have binoculars. Honey, they just zero in on everything."

"I'll shave, Renee. Is that all?" I got up off the La-Z-Boy to hang the phone up.

"Yes. Well, no. I thought since you and Sparkle were such good friends, I'd make yall one of the bathing suit pairs. It'll be you and her, and two other girls doing the whole summer lineup. Okay?"

What could I say to that?

Suddenly Renee wasn't my hero anymore. Somehow knowing I could trick her with the fake contract dropped her into the ocean of nobodies for me. She didn't care about me. She didn't think I was ever going to amount to anything.

She had more enthusiasm for a dog. It really bothered me that she had kicked me out for nothing and taken me back in for money. I guess most people are like that, but it seems like your heroes should be different. I'd have to get a new one, was all.

Almost as soon as I hung up, the phone rang again.

"Dixie? Is this Dixie? Obviously violent behavior runs in your family," screamed Sparkle.

"What are you talking about?" I asked her. I tugged the phone cord back to the La-Z-Boy.

She said, "Oh, don't go playing dumb on me. I'm standing here at the Speeds' one minute, the next I'm at Momma's putting a steak on her eye. Don't tell me you don't know what I'm talking about."

"Sparkle, I have no idea what you're talking about. Not a clue."

She slammed the phone down. I couldn't tell if she'd hung up or not, but then she picked it back up. "Your mother went over to my mother's house and beat her up. I had to bring her back to Buck's she was so upset. Momma Speed's in the bedroom with her now trying to calm her nerves." She said this loud, as if the entire Speed family had congregated to listen to her every word.

"That's just too bad, Spark. What'd she hit her for?" I didn't understand.

"Hit her? Let me tell you something, Dixie Riggs. Your momma didn't just hit her, she pulverized her."

"Sparkle, listen, I'm sorry about your mom, but as far as what goes on between our mothers, I think we'd better stay out of it." I leaned all the way back in LeDaire's La-Z-Boy and looked out the curtains. Her car wasn't in the driveway. I couldn't figure out what was going on. "Besides, they probably got in a fight over that dumb Johnny D. Did Trina tell you what it was about?"

"No, she wouldn't speak to anyone. She was too upset."

"Well, let's you and me work on our problems and let them work on theirs."

Sparkle didn't say anything for a moment. Then she said, "Why are you being so nice?"

I said, "Because Renee says you and me are pairing up at the fashion show. We might as well try and get along."

She was quiet again. Then she said, "Oh, I get it. You're trying to weazle Buck back, aren't you? But for your information, that will never happen. He's asked me to marry him. He said he wanted a woman he could count on. Didn't you Buck?"

I heard Buck in the background mumbling something. My heart dropped.

"What we don't want around here anymore," she continued, "is more trouble from you. Frankly, Dixie, I don't know if me or Buck could ever trust you again, what with all you've done."

Oooooh, flames were shooting through my body. But, as nicely as I could, I said, "Sparkle, honey, the last thing you have to worry about is me. Rest assured, everything is over between me and Buck. All I want right now is for you and me to salvage what little friendship we have left."

This softened her up some. Not completely. I had to eat more crow and more crow. Finally she gave in and said, "Well, okay. Maybe we can try and start over. Is your car still busted up? I can give you a ride if it is."

It wasn't. Lou had gotten it from Wing's and spent the entire morning putting in brand-new hoses. She was purring now. "Yeah it's still broken. A ride would be nice."

"Well me and Buck will be there tomorrow. Don't keep us waiting. It'll be nice to see you again. You know, I've missed you, Dixie. You sure this is okay?"

I said, "Let me just put it to you this way. You can always find another man in your life, but it's rare to find a girl you can talk to. It's like I always told you, Sparkle. You and me have got to stick together if we're going to make it in this world. You can count on me."

"You mean it, Dixie?"

"With all my heart, Spark. With all my heart."

Momma and Daddy Speed drove. Buck and Sparkle were in the backseat. Sparkle fixed it so I couldn't sit by Buck. She sat in the middle, closer to me, so she could squeeze me up to the window. She wasn't going to give me an inch with him.

Buck, on the other hand, wouldn't have cared anyway. He just kept staring out the window like his daddy. Momma Speed, of course, sat up front and prattled along about the trees being so green this summer and wasn't it a good day to be on the beach and my, how the traffic was getting so thick these days. In general, the women talked and the men looked miserable. Your typical Saturday outing.

The Newberry's fashion show was being held out on the beach, on a grand stage built especially for the show. The wind was whipping around. The June sun was blazing. The tide was high, the mood was up and about forty of Myrtle Beach's finest lookers, men and women, were standing behind the stage, getting dressed. We went and found Renee. She gave us our first outfits. Then she told us to go on backstage and she took Sparkle aside, but not before Sparkle first gave Buck a warning look, and me, all her bags.

It was the first chance Buck and me had alone together since he'd left me at the hotel. And he wouldn't even talk to me. I could have told him right then about Sparkle being in the porno pictures. I never had before, because at the time he'd already hated her too much. I hadn't wanted him to hate her any more. But now there wasn't a reason left in the world to protect her. But I knew if I told him now, he'd just think I was trying to make trouble. He'd never believe me. So after five minutes of sounding like Momma Speed, I said, "Buck, I can see you don't want to have a thing to do with me. But let me ask you this. What if this is your baby I've got in my stomach? Are you just going to up and leave me?"

He stopped and looked at me. "Dixie Riggs, I don't plan on leaving you dirt poor if that's my baby. But first we've got to find out. I guess that's going to take some time, isn't it?"

"Buck," I said. "It just has to be yours. I love you. A woman just can't love a man as much as I do you and not get pregnant by him. I know all my hormones were going overtime wanting a baby that looked just like you."

"Sure, and what about Donnie?"

"Well, I don't know. You didn't want me. He did."

Buck got furious. "Well, that's not the issue. It's all that other cheating and lying and stealing. A preacher can't be having no wife like that." He started walking fast then, too fast, and I couldn't have caught up with him unless I'd ran.

When I got to the backstage dressing room, I immediately began to go through Sparkle's makeup bag, pulling out her bottle of hairspray, emptying some of it out, and filling the rest back up with baby oil. It was a trick one of the *Playboy* bunnies in one of Daddy Speed's catalogs had said she used once in a beauty contest. Any minute Sparkle would come back to remove the scarf over the curlers in her hair. Then she'd take out her curling clips and curlers and spray her hair good and long, as Renee had instructed. In this weather, hairspray was a must. I had mixed just enough oil and lacquer that the lacquer would hold until Sparkle got up onstage and the hot sun came beating down on her head.

The ideas kept coming to me. I'd screw with both pairs of her shoes. I'd pull the heels out just so far. I'd put a run, where she couldn't see it, in every pair of her hose; they'd start at the heel, then work their way up the entire length of the leg as she did her first three-quarter French military turn. Yes indeedy, I would spritz her powder compact with the new hairspray mix, and hope there would be enough oil to activate the powder in such a way that it would turn her face a nice splotchy orange when the sun hit her. And nobody ever said I couldn't add a little oil to her mascara, too. I was just pushing the brush in and out and in and out of the tube, mixing it up, when Sparkle arrived, saying, "Just what in the hell do you think you're doing?"

I said, "Using your makeup. You got a problem with that?" I asked, as I started to apply her mascara on my lashes.

"Nah, can you fix my hair?"

I said, "Me? Be delighted to. Where's Trina and her hair tools?"

She said, "She'll be along later. She still doesn't feel so good since your momma got to her. Listen, I've got something to tell you." She looked around to see if anyone could hear her. "Guess what Renee told me, and I'm not supposed to breathe a word of it."

I said, "What?" as one by one I took out her rollers and combed her hair. I did a little back brushing and then sprayed and sprayed with my new version of her Final Net hairspray.

She said, "Well, you know, it just so happens that Renee already has a talent scout ready to pick up me and Buck."

I sprayed some more. "Is that so?"

She whipped around and looked up at me. "I swear, Dixie. Everything's happening so fast for us." She patted my hand to get me to spray more.

"Yes, it is, isn't it," I said, spraying.

"Boy, we're going to be famous, me and Buck," she said, jumping up to hug me. "Buck's going to go crazy when he hears we've got an agent."

"Sit down," I said, and I sprayed the front and the back and the sides of her hair again.

"Hey, isn't that enough already?" she asked.

"I suppose so," I said, spraying her bangs one final time.

"Anyway, you and I won't be a pair anymore. She's put you with Dorothy Newberry, the daughter of the owner. Renee wants me to go on last so everyone will remember me.

Well, go on, honey," Sparkle said. "You need to get yourself done."

"I'm done," I said, undoing my robe to reveal a bright yellow one-piece with a silver chain belt.

She patted my stomach. "You've got a cute little body. Hey, you don't think you're going to, well, you know, show or anything?" she asked, slipping in her red polka-dotted French-cut one-piece.

"Lord, let's hope not," I said, putting on my high heels.

"If I do say so myself, I look good." She pressed at the sides of her hair without really touching it, so she wouldn't mess it up. Then she grabbed her shoes.

"Hey," I said. "Let me borrow those things since you're not going on until last." I didn't want her finding out they were broken just yet.

She looked at me funny and shrugged her shoulders. "Okay," she said, and walked away.

The nerve, was what I thought. Friendships were like bathing suits. When you found a good one, it fit just perfectly until *bam!* one day you'd put it on and for no apparent reason it wouldn't fit at all. And oh how I hated thinking this way. I was always comparing men to things like socks or chairs, and friends to bathing suits, and mothers to TVs or tables or TV tables, sounding like a weirdo, making hardly any sense at all. And if I wasn't doing that, I was comparing myself to everything moving, like the bitch who modeled a bikini in front of me with a body that made mine look like a backyard weed.

The woman was unbelievable. First, she got up onstage, wearing a real floor-length mink stole. Then she took it off and handed it to one of the talent scouts. Her body looked like she had oiled it for days. Then, after smiling a killer smile at each individual scout, she began twirling around, dancing to the beat of the music on the loudspeakers. Then, there I was, where she had been, watching everyone watching her still walking away. All except for some piggy looking man who couldn't take his eyes off my feet. He was short and greasy looking and probably Mr. Newberry, himself, wondering how I got up onstage with such disgusting looking feet. I hadn't done a thing with them for a month. One rule in modeling is: Always make sure your fingernails and toenails are kept neat and orderly.

Well, I had to follow this woman with the gorgeous body three more times up onstage, each time with the same result. The last time, that horrid little man came running up to me, talking so fast and in some kind of foreign language that I wasn't about to give him the time of day. And he smelled awful, like old spaghetti sauce. I pushed him away from me and said, "Get lost, mister."

Then Sparkle came out for her first grand walk up the steps onto the stage. I slipped her the shoes and she slipped them on. She was smiling. Then she squinted and rocked her ankle back and forth and looked down at her shoe. And then some girl behind her gave her a little nudge and she started up the steps, still kind of smiling, but looking unsure of her step.

"*Lalacolla beneccio,*" said the man, or something like that. I didn't understand him.

He grabbed my arm. I pushed him off and said, "I told you to get lost, buddy. Now move it."

I don't like being rude to anyone, but I had to get a closer look at Sparkle. I had to get closer to the stage. Suddenly I saw her. There she was, hobbling, and the wind was whipping her hair around into one great big clompy strand around her oily face. And she wasn't smiling.

The little piggy man came right back up to me and said more gibberish and that's when I saw LeDaire. She was standing by the exit ramp. She was holding on to Momma Speed who was pulling on a reluctant Daddy Speed. Everything happened so fast. Faster than fast. Sparkle came down off the stage. She looked at me. I looked at her. The little man grabbed my arm again. LeDaire grabbed Sparkle's arm, then pushed her up against the wall. Daddy Speed just stood there, like Momma Speed, who stood there looking confused and nice, like she wanted to be somewhere else but was too polite to say so.

Then Buck came over. In his tuxedo he looked like a movie star. He said, "What's going on here?"

LeDaire pulled something out of her pocketbook and

waved it in his face. "You, young man, owe my daughter a big apology."

He shook his head, still confused. "Let me see that."

I couldn't make it out. Sparkle screamed and tried to grab it. All the while this crazy little man who spoke no English kept clutching my arm.

"Leave me alone, I tell you. Get away from me," I said. I pushed him away and walked up to Buck to see what he had. We were both looking at the naked pictures of Sparkle Starling. Buck's face went as white as the ruffled shirt he was wearing.

Sparkle started crying. She started screaming. "Give me those! I want those back!"

LeDaire said, "No honey. You and your momma have had them long enough. It's time to share."

I said, "But I don't understand."

Buck was confused, too. "What's going on here?"

LeDaire said, "You see, Buck darling, Dixie had told me that Sparkle and her momma weren't speaking, only every time I went out with Trina, all she did, all night long, was brag about her little girl. Sparkle this and Sparkle that until I was sick to death of hearing it. And I thought to myself, this is not a woman who is mad at her child. So when Dixie told me about Sparkle hating you and then planning to marry you, well, it just all came together." She took the pictures out of Buck's hand and threw them at Sparkle and hissed, "This little snake and her mother have been planning this thing for months. Whatever Sparkle wants, Sparkle gets. And this time she wanted you, Buck. It was that damn simple."

The foreign man tugged at my arm, but I hardly noticed. All I could say was, "How did you know, Momma? How come I didn't?"

Momma said, "Honey, because you were in love with Buck. I wasn't. And you loved Sparkle. I didn't know anything about her. All I knew was that her mother tried to steal my Johnny D. away from me one night and it was like, okay. I get it. Like mother like daughter. So I beat the shit out of her and got the whole story."

Everyone was quiet. Sparkle was crying. Buck was just

looking at me. Momma Speed grabbed me up in her arms and said, “Now maybe I can go back home and finish that cross-stitching I started,” and she winked at me.

LeDaire pushed Sparkle against the wall again. “The next time you think about fucking around with my little girl, you little slut, I’ll beat the shit out of you. As for you, Buck,” she said, turning to him, “maybe you’ve got some things to talk over with Dixie?”

The audience was clapping for the male models, modeling sports clothes. Some skinny man came up and told Buck to get in place. He was up next. He looked beaten. He looked like he wanted to look at me, only it would hurt him to.

Sparkle was still crying.

Daddy Speed was just standing there looking disgusted by everyone.

Momma Speed took Buck by the hand. “My poor, sweet son can’t see past his own eyes. I always knew you were a good girl, Dixie. Didn’t I always say that, Daddy? Didn’t I always tell you that you were wrong about her?”

Daddy Speed mumbled something.

“Just ignore him, Dixie,” she said. “He’ll come around. He always does.”

I said, “But what about the credit card? I treated you so bad.”

Momma Speed laughed. “Dear child, if my son didn’t have any more sense than to bring you into our home and not marry you or give you any allowance or nothing, I can hardly blame you for trying to find happiness somewhere else.” She hugged me. “You can always use my credit cards. Only, next time, let’s try to hit more sales, huh?” She patted me on the behind, something she would never do any other time, and said, “Come on, Daddy. Let’s leave these kids alone. And get that look off your face.”

“Hold on,” LeDaire called after them. “I’m coming with you. I want to talk some sense into that husband of yours.”

“Well come on then,” said Momma Speed, laughing. “Talking sense into this man is a bigger job than I can handle alone.”

As soon as they left Sparkle tried to talk to Buck but he

told her to shut up. And then, I don't know, it's stupid I guess. It's just that when you know someone's about to apologize to you and you know you're in the right, that maybe it's the first time you've ever been in the right in your entire life, you can get just so damned embarrassed. So what do you think I did? You wouldn't have liked it, but I ran off the other way.

I was still wearing the last bathing suit, this shiny black deal with gold coins sewn all over everywhere. I threw off my shoes and ran as fast and as hard as I could to the ocean. And I jumped in. The water felt so good. All my cares vanished but one, Sparkle. It was funny. I hated seeing her crying like that, with her hair all oily and hobbling on those shoes. No matter what she had done to me, I loved that girl. Maybe it was the new mother in me. Maybe it was just that it was so damned hard to find a girl as fun to be around as Sparkle Starling.

I swam and swam and the water felt so cool, so safe. I wondered if that was what my baby felt like inside my tummy. I began to feel good all over. Up until then, I had never really decided on keeping this baby. But the water just felt so good. I rode wave after wave in, and swam out for more, and finally I rode my last wave in only to find that piggy little man standing at the water's edge, sweating and pulling a shoe out of his jacket. He was holding it out for me. He started shaking it at me and pointing at my feet and saying, "*Coccaliocacha, ladadaddaddooo*," or whatever it was he was saying.

I shook my head like a dog, making sure to get him all wet. And you know what? He didn't care. He just stood there holding that stupid shoe out for me.

I went up to him and put my face right up to his, my little nose pushing up against his big one, and screamed, "What?! What is it that you want?"

And very slowly, in the worst English I have possibly ever heard, he said, "Shoe to wear you for."

I slapped the shit out of him. It was one thing, posing in nudies with my friend for fun, but to have some little creep come up with a pair of shoes for me to wear so he could get his little jollies off, that was another thing altogether.

I slapped him again just to be sure he knew I wasn't a hooker.

But he didn't budge. He kept that shoe out and said, "Shoe to wear you for. Shoe to wear you for. Beautiful feet."

"Mister, let me get this straight," I said, pointing at the shoe. "I just slapped you and you still want me to try that shoe on?"

He got all excited, pushing the shoe up against my shoulder. "*Si! Si!*"

"Okay, mister," I said, grabbing the shoe from him and plopping down on the sand. "I'll put this shoe on if you promise to leave me alone afterwards. Deal?" He gave me a long string of excited dribble I couldn't have understood if someone had paid me to.

I looked up at the stage. Buck was nowhere. It was funny, but seeing it so empty now, it was hard to tell that anything had just happened up there, including the show, and Buck and all that stuff. It looked peaceful. Everything felt peaceful, too. Once again the tide was going down and the sun was just beginning to give her afternoon Easter parade, with her pink and orange and purple ribbons of clouds streaming across the Myrtle Beach sky.

The little man sat down in his suit, right on the wet sand next to me, and waited and didn't say a word. So I smiled at him. And he smiled at me and looked at my foot and nodded. The shoe went on just as pretty as you please, and I'd never seen a man so happy. That foreign guy just glowed. Without saying another word, he pulled another shoe from out of his inside jacket pocket and handed that to me too.

Now I am here to tell you that these were not pretty shoes. They were brown. They looked like something Robin Hood wore. But when I slipped that second shoe on and it fit so perfectly it felt like an impression of my foot in the sand, that little man knocked himself onto his back, in his suit, right on that wet sand, and started clasping his hands together and shaking them at the setting sun and laughing until I was laying back laughing with him. And you know what? I didn't even know what we were laughing about. I was just glad we were, was all.

He wouldn't let me take the shoes off. I mean, of course I could have taken them off, but every time I tried to he'd start waving his arms around like a fool. He was cracking me up. And when it started getting cold and I started making my way back to the stage, squeezing myself for warmth, he took his coat off and put it around my shoulders. Then he pulled out a bottle of wine. Well, I thought it was wine, but it tasted like Jergens lotion smelled, and it made everything nice and soft and warm, so we sat back down on the sand and drank some together. It was called Nocello. It had a walnut glued onto the top of the cork. Drinking it made me happy while I watched the Myrtle Beach boys take the stage down.

The fashion show was over and now the regular nightly show of the neon lights took their turn lighting up the sky: solid red ones, being circled by yellow blinking ones and circling blue and green ones. FOOT-LONG HOT DOGS! HOME OF THE DOUBLE DOG! GAMES! GAMES! GAMES! ARCADE! ARCADE! ARCADE! GIRLS! GIRLS! GIRLS! all lit up the Myrtle Beach sky.

And I said to the little man, "Don't you think it's pretty? Don't you think that in its own seedy way, Myrtle Beach is a pretty little town?"

He just looked at me and didn't say a word. Then he

pointed to my feet again, like he'd been doing off and on ever since we'd sat down to drink. Then he clasped his hands again, shaking them to the stars up in the heavens.

It's funny, but I was never scared of this man. Even when it was that dark, and we were on the beach alone, I was not afraid of him. I mean, he could have been a rapist or a murderer or, worse, some crazy cult leader trying to abduct me into one of those rose-selling religions where I wouldn't get to eat for days. But I trusted this man. There was something very peaceful going on between us. I couldn't put my finger on it. Maybe it was because we were misfits together.

I said, "Hey, has anyone ever told you how fat you were?" just to see if it would rattle him. I needed some sign that he could understand what I was saying. I figured calling someone fat was always a good ticket to get them riled up. He looked at me and grinned and nodded his head like an idiot. This man could not speak word one of English.

When I said, "What country are you from?"

He answered back by pointing to my shoes and saying, "*Si! Si!*" and stretching his arms out like he was a flying plane. He did this two or three times together real fast so I could get the picture, but I couldn't get the picture. I figured it was time to find someone I could load this jerk off on. I couldn't leave him all alone, stranded on the beach, that was for sure. Someone would probably take his wallet if I did.

We finished the Nocello and I reached into the jacket he'd given me to wear. I found a pen, an empty book of Newberry Department Store matches, but no wallet. There was nothing in there to clue me in on where he was from.

I said, "Hey. You got a wallet?"

And he grinned.

"A wallet?" I said again, motioning to his pants pocket.

He still didn't get it. There was no sense in wasting my time.

I didn't want to throw the bottle away. It was so beautiful. So instead I held up my hand and said, "Wait here," and walked back to the water.

He followed me anyway.

We sat down on the wet sand again, and I opened the book of matches and pressed it against his back, and wrote on the inside: *Buck, I will love you forever. Your Dixie girl.*

I kissed it, then wound it into a tube, stuck it in the bottle, and capped the bottle shut. Then I walked into the water and threw it as far as I could. If it didn't come back to land, it was a good sign. If it did, well, I was used to bad luck.

It stayed out on the water, bobbing up and down with the waves. I stood on that shore, holding my pregnant tummy, and watched it float away.

Finally, when I couldn't see it anymore, I grabbed the man by the arm and led him up the beach to the Ocean Highway. I needed to get a ride home. I needed to thank LeDaire for coming through for me. I was so proud she was my momma.

We walked past the stage, past the workers taking it down, past the places where the talent scouts had sat. I wondered if Sparkle and Buck were still together after all was said and done. We walked onto the parking lot where the pay phones were. Every so often the foreigner would stop me and point at my feet, smiling.

"Yes, yes," I'd say, smiling back, nodding.

"*Si! Si!*" he'd say, clapping his hands to his chin.

It didn't take a genius to figure out that Sparkle had been there. I guess she figured I'd be calling someone, because right next to the phones, right in a handicapped parking spot, lay my change of clothes and my fake rabbit fur coat. They'd been driven over. And they were wet. There was a note with Sparkle's handwriting on it that I didn't even bother to read. I was looking at the photographs, the ones of her naked. The ones I'd taken of her. The ones that, up until now, no one but me had ever seen.

I turned to the man and said, "Where are you staying?"

And he pointed at my feet.

"Yeah. Yeah. Boy, we've got to find somebody who can speak your language."

He wasn't sick, so I couldn't take him to the hospital. And I knew no Myrtle Beach policeman could understand a word he said. So I decided I'd go find Reno. Reno could help me out. Reno could always help me out. That was the good thing about Reno. He was from New Jersey. I figured anyone from New Jersey must know Spanish. So me and the man, who I was now calling Buster Brown because he kept pointing at my feet every five minutes, walked all the way down the end of the boardwalk until we came upon the Tiger Alley Saloon, and I said, "Wait here."

When I started to go in, he grabbed my arm frantically, yelling, *"Commociallo bellicimo!"* or something to that effect.

"Okay, okay," I said. "Calm down. Calm down. Come on in then."

But still, he would not let go of me. He held on to my arm tight, like a lost child, as I went to find Reno.

Finding Reno is never hard. The trick is to find the girl. Not some smartass type girl who'd give him a hard time, but some girl who looked like she needed money real bad. The only one like that in the whole place was sitting alone at the bar. I stared at her not knowing what my next move would be, and then up comes Reno, out from the bathroom, pulling a bar stool up next to her. Bingo! I thought. Right on the money, I thought.

"Reno," I said.

He turned around. "Hey Dixie. What's up? Contract work out okay?"

I said, "Hey," to the girl, and then to Reno, "Like a jewel. Renee signed me up for her agency right away. She gets ten percent of everything. Listen, can you speak Spanish? This guy's Spanish or something, and he won't leave me alone."

Reno reached out and shook the guy's hand. He said something to him that didn't seem to register. Then he said something else and the man started jumping up and down going crazy talking. Reno put his hand up and said, "Not so fast, not so fast," and then he shook his head and said something in Buster Brown's language. That's when Buster Brown started talking real slow, pointing at my feet the whole time. Then he took his wallet out and gave Reno a business card and some money.

"Whoa, whoa," said Reno. "Not so fast there." Then he talked more foreign talk to the man. A lot more.

I ordered another beer. "What's he saying, Reno? What's all that *andiamatta* junk mean?"

"That's *andiamo*, Dixie. He's saying, 'Let's go! 'Let's go!' "

"Oh." I sipped my beer. I was getting cold sitting there in my wet bathing suit. "Where does he want to go?"

"Hold on. Let me hear what he's got to say."

So Reno listened and I waited. The little man kept grabbing my feet and pulling out his wallet all at the same time. He was frantic, desperate.

I was freezing. I turned to talk to the girl but she didn't want to talk. She didn't even want me in the same room with her. The man picked up my foot again and pushed it hard at Reno.

"Hey, quit already, would you?" I said.

And Reno said, "Honey. Watch your step. It looks like you're coming into some big money after all. This man's from the shoe district in Italy and he wants to give you a contract. And you know what?" Reno said, as he flagged down the bartender. "He just gave me a thousand bucks to prove he means it. He thinks I'm your agent. Hey bartender," Reno said. "A bottle of your best champagne."

The bartender poured out glasses full and Reno toasted the air. "*Saremo ricchi,*" he said. "We're all going to be rich."

"*Sarà una diva!*" the Italian said, toasting me.

"What's that? What's that mean, Reno?" I asked.

Reno squeezed the back of my neck and put his forehead against mine. "It means, Dixie Riggs, that you're going to be a star. It means your dreams are finally coming true after all."

43

Seven and a half months have passed by this time and I have been to Italy. I have worn some of the most expensive shoes in the world. I have had shoes molded from my very feet that some of the richest ladies in New York City have bought from Saks Fifth Avenue and Bergdorf Goodman, places I never even knew existed up until now. You can even find me in the pages of *Vogue* magazine. If you see a pair of shoes, those are probably my feet.

I look at those famous feet now, sticking out of a pair of cheap Kmart mules—just a little something my momma sent me for the plane trip back home—and I see my slim ankles. They never did bloat up like LeDaire said. I must have inherited the ankles of the Muff Man. And maybe I'll have a little girl who will inherit them, too. Little girl, little boy, it doesn't matter. I am going to have this baby. And I am so big I'm going to be lucky if I don't have it on this plane.

I sip a nice cool whiskey sour and feel just a little guilty about it, since one of my shoe ads was opposite a page that said that alcohol was bad for the unborn child. But so is all this flying around, even if it is in first class, and I still have to catch two more planes. I might as well be relaxed about it.

The Italy to New York connection touches down without a hitch, but it is here that everything falls apart. The New

York to Atlanta is boarding and I have to catch one of those special little golf cart things reserved especially for the disabled or old or very pregnant, like myself, to make it. And wouldn't you know it. Just like in my dreams. There, taking the last boarding pass and following the last passenger up the walkway onto the plane, is Paulette, Buck's old girl. My heart is beating and I can feel my pulse all the way from my skinny ankles up to my humongous stomach. And I am thinking, this cannot possibly be true. Surely I am not about to meet Paulette for the first time, fat.

My face flushes as the man drives me up the ramp, up to the plane, and I am searching, searching frantically for that woman. But I do not see her anywhere. I do not even know if she knows that I ever existed. But I do know that the minute she sees me, she will be able to tell I was once Buck's girl. I do not know how I know this I just believe it to be true. I plop down into my first-class seat like a real fatso, right next to a man and his cigar, and order myself up another whiskey sour. Then I turn my head to the window and look out and wait for takeoff.

I will not think about this. I will not think about any of it. Not the strong letter of proposal Buck sent me, or the weak one Donnie broke down and sent me, not even all the letters of apology I've gotten from Sparkle, who, by the way, is now the head hairstylist at Trina's shop. And I won't think about Paulette, either. I will wait until I'm on that little puddle jumper that connects from Atlanta to Myrtle Beach, and then, then I will think about it all. I will let it all rush over me like a tidal wave on that small plane with not possibly enough room for all the luggage I've managed to bring back with me. I've brought Buck and Donnie both back a snazzy pair of expensive Italian shoes. I bought LeDaire and Lou back matching leather coats. I even brought Sparkle back something. I brought her back a fake rabbit fur coat, just like the one I used to have that she stole from me so long ago. I even brought something back for Momma and Daddy Speed, first, because they forgave me for the Visa card stuff, and second, because he is busy building my baby a crib and rocker, and because she is knitting it all the little booties it could need for a whole baby lifetime.

And this will be a good Christian baby. God will smile down on it, just like He smiles down on me, and get it through all the gray areas, just like He did for me.

Suddenly, out of the corner of my eye, I see Paulette closing the first-class curtains. Her hair is a beautiful sleek brown and it swings just so as she turns around, and I turn around, away from her. It's really very stupid, but in the end, after it's all said and done, even though I've never even met her before, I like her better than Buck or Donnie or Sparkle all rolled into one. Through it all, she's the one that's been my best friend. She's the one who I've counted on the most to help me rise above all my problems. It was Paulette who was on my mind when I decided I was going to be better than what I used to be. If it wasn't for her, I wouldn't have had the hunger. I wouldn't have gotten that six-figure income coming at me all year long for the next five years. If it wasn't for her I wouldn't be a famous shoe model. So there is no way, with me this fat, this big, this huge, this pregnant, that I will look her square in the face.

Someone touches me on the shoulder and offers me my drink and I smile up to say thanks. But instead I just nod. The girl is the one I thought was Paulette. Only it isn't her. And I know it's really corny, but suddenly I realize I'm coming to a happy ending. Everything's going to be all right. I don't have to answer Buck's letter right away. Things can wait. Everything can wait. There's no hurry on this stuff. This baby is going to have a good life. It will either have great blond hair, like Donnie, or it's going to have great curly brown hair, like Buck. Glory, it doesn't take a genius to see how lucky I am. Just think, right now I could be working down on the Myrtle Beach boardwalk as a salesgirl at the Gay Dolphin, or selling double dogs to the tourists, trying to keep my baby in clean diapers. "Whew!" is what I think. "Just think," is what I think. "For a while there, all I wanted was Buck," is what I think. Well, you know what I think now? I think it's just like in *Gone With the Wind*, where

Scarlett O'Hara says she'll be better off thinking about it tomorrow. After all, there's no rush on these things. Oh, there might be some kind of a rush, but not a rush, rush. You know what I mean?

I mean, it's something like what I'm thinking right this very minute. Like about me and Buck, and all that stuff I had to go through to get him back, and what I'm going to do now that I've got him. I mean, do I really want him after all this? In the end, when all is said and done, is it really worth it? I just can't help but to wonder about it all, to wonder what it's all about. Because, you know, it's like sometimes I think women's biggest problem is, they get all excited over nothing, and then they marry it.